LAWFULLY REDEEMED

A K-9 LAWKEEPER BOOK

LORANA HOOPES

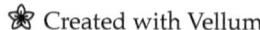

This book is dedicated to all the hardworking law enforcement officers out there. Our world would not be as safe without all of you.

And to my family who lets me sacrifice time with them to write these stories in my head.

NOTE FROM THE AUTHOR

Thank you so much for picking up this book. I hope you enjoy the story and the characters as they are dear to my heart. If you do, please leave a review at your retailer. It really does make a difference because it lets people make an informed decision about books. Below are the other books in this series. I would love for you to check them out. I'd also like to offer you a sample of my newest book. This will sign you up for my newsletter which allows me to send you weekly emails with news and promotional information about my books, but you are welcome to cancel any time. Free Sample!

Lawkeepers series:
Lawfully Justified

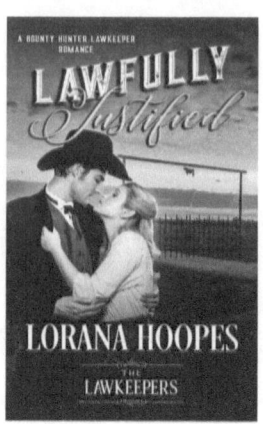

Lawfully Matched

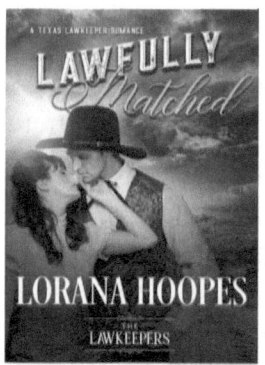

The Scarlet Wedding

Lawfully Pursued

C alvin stared at the computer screen and rubbed his eyes. While he loved his job, the monotony sometimes got to him. Day in and day out, just him and his computer. He could really use some company.

A knock sounded at the door, and Calvin chuckled at the timing. His good mood faded, however, as he opened the door and tried to suppress his sigh. His brother Chris stood on the other side, and from the slight twitching of his body, Calvin could tell he was using again.

"What is it, Chris?" Calvin hated the tone in his voice, but he had been bailing Chris out of trouble for the last few years.

Chris hadn't always been this way. During his Junior year of college, their father was diagnosed with cancer. After a tough yearlong battle, the cancer won. Two months after that, a car accident took their mother's life. It had been too much for twenty-two-year-old Chris to bear. Heck, it had been too much for Calvin to bear at twenty-six, but at least he'd had a job to fall back on. A solitary, retreat-from-everyone kind of job, but still a job. Chris, on the other hand, hadn't quite finished college, having taken time off when their father got sick, and therefore wasn't sure where to go.

Unfortunately, he turned to drugs. At first, it had just been smoking marijuana at parties, which was legal in their state. Then, it had transitioned into smoking pot every night. From there, Chris turned to harder drugs like ecstasy and Oxycodone. Now, Calvin believed Chris was dabbling in cocaine or heroin, but he couldn't bring himself to ask. Ignorance wasn't really blissful, but it kept him from going completely crazy with guilt.

Chris twitched and rubbed his nose. "I just need a couple hundred dollars, Calvin. Enough to get me through the month. The landlord raised the rent again."

Calvin knew this was a lie. Chris had already used this excuse, along with losing his job, having to repair his car, and getting robbed. No, this money was for drugs and Calvin was done supplying his habit. Last month when Chris asked for money, he promised to attend rehab. Either he had not fulfilled that promise, or it hadn't worked for him.

"I'm sorry, Chris, but I'm not giving you any more money." As hard as it was to watch his little brother go down this path, he needed some tough love. Calvin reached for the door handle to shut the front door, but Chris managed to wiggle his toe in to keep it from closing.

"Food then?" he asked with another slight twitch. "I haven't eaten in a few days. Can I at least have some food?"

Calvin knew he should say no, but this was his brother and he couldn't watch him starve to death. "Fine," he said, stepping back and allowing Chris to open the door. "Lunch, but that's it. Then you leave."

"You got it. Thanks, Cal, you always were a great brother."

Calvin sighed. He wished he could just be a brother instead of his brother's keeper. "Have a seat," Calvin said, pointing to the living room couch. "I'll make a sandwich and pack you an extra one for later."

Chris nodded and grabbed the remote as he plopped down on Calvin's couch.

Calvin continued to the kitchen and grabbed the bread, meat, and cheese from the fridge. The sound of some football game carried across the room as he prepared the sandwiches. With a sigh, he thought back to high school. Back to a simpler time when Chris played football and his biggest worry was getting a date on Friday night.

What would it take to get Chris back on track? Calvin wasn't sure he could handle any more loss. If he lost Chris, he'd be all alone, but though he'd been praying for the last two years, God hadn't answered his prayer yet.

He grabbed two bags of chips from the pantry and added them to the plates. Then he sealed the third sandwich in a bag and placed it on Chris's plate.

"You weren't watching the game?" Chris asked when Calvin entered the living room. For a moment, his eyes shone bright and clear.

"No, I was working," Calvin said. As a developer for a software company, he often worked from home and his work time and personal time mixed together frequently. "But I'll watch it with you now." He handed Chris his plate and then sat beside him, placing his own plate on his lap.

"Thanks, bro," Chris said, opening the bag of chips and shoving three in his mouth. "They're down by a touchdown, but they might be able to pull it out," he said around his mouthful of food.

Calvin bit back a smile. It was nice to see Chris as he remembered him even if it only lasted an hour or so. As he bit into his own sandwich, he sent another prayer heavenward. *"Lord, please reach Chris. Help him get clean and see the error of his ways before he ends up dead."*

Chris's sandwich and chips were gone before the first commercial break. Calvin would have made more, but Chris didn't ask. When the game ended, Chris tucked the extra sandwich in his jacket pocket as he stood up to leave.

"Hey, Calvin," he said, digging the toe of his shoe into the carpet. "If I needed help, not financial, but, you know, other help, would you be there for me?"

The stress on the word other led Calvin to believe Chris was asking for help in hiding, making, or selling drugs. All things Calvin would never do. He sucked in a deep breath as he thought about his answer. "I love you Chris, I do, but I won't do anything illegal, not even for you."

Chris nodded, his shaggy brown hair swishing against his pale skin. "Yeah, I got it. Thanks for the food though."

"You're welcome."

After one final awkward stare, Chris shuffled to the front door. As the door closed behind him, Calvin leaned against it and sighed. Giving tough love was not easy, and he hoped he was doing the right thing.

2

"What are you doing, DP?"

Dani Higgins stopped her jiggling leg and sat up. "I'm just anxious, you know? I wish we had a case. Sydney here is ready to work." She reached down and patted the head of the German Shepherd at her side.

Danielle, or Dani as her fellow officers called her except for Aaron who insisted on using her initials, had recently transferred into the K-9 unit. Her dog, Sydney, had just graduated. Neither had showed off their skills yet, but both girls were ready.

Aaron Jones, her training partner, shook his grey-streaked head. "When you've been at this job as long as I have, you'll enjoy the time when nothing crazy is going on."

"Mount up, you two," Lieutenant Craig said, entering their area.

"What's going on?" Aaron asked.

"A drug deal gone bad left us with one body at an abandoned warehouse and one name, a Chris Phillips. We're headed to his place and we want the dogs along to sniff for drugs," Lieutenant Craig answered.

Dani tried hard not to smile as she grabbed her gear and Sydney's leash. "We're on it, Lieutenant," she said.

"Try not to look too excited," Aaron said to Dani as they climbed into the SUV.

"Oh, come on, this will be an easy case," Dani said as she strapped into her seatbelt. She had ridden with Aaron enough to determine a seatbelt was never optional. "Find some drugs, bust the perp, and call it a day."

Aaron shook his head. "They're never as easy as they seem," he said.

They arrived at the house a few minutes later. A small rambler with peeling paint and a yard that looked like it hadn't been touched in years, the house exuded a feeling of sadness. Two other police cars sat on the street in front of the house.

"I guess drugs don't always pay," Dani said, unbuckling her seatbelt and tucking a strand of her blonde hair behind her ears. She opened the door and walked to the rear of the car to get Sydney and Aaron's dog, Dexter, out of the back.

"Follow my lead," Aaron said, taking the leash from Dani. He led the way up the overgrown pathway and to the sagging porch which appeared in dire need of repair. Another officer stood just inside the open door.

"Come on in," he said, "but watch your step. The house hasn't been well taken care of."

Dani and Aaron led the dogs carefully into the house. "Okay, girl," Dani said, leaning down to Sydney. "We are looking for drugs. Go find them."

Sydney sniffed the floor. At the hall closet, she pawed and whined. "There might be drugs in here," Dani shouted to her fellow officers. She opened the door slowly and Sydney nosed her way in, pushing piles of clothes around on the floor. After a few seconds, she backed out of the small space, a large brick of marijuana in her mouth. Much more than allowed for recreational use.

"Good girl," Dani said, patting the dog and rewarding her with a quick tug of war with her towel.

The towel was actually how Sydney was trained to sniff drugs. Dani began with just the white towel, clean and devoid of scent. They would play tug of war until Sydney got tired. Then Dani would wrap the towel around some marijuana and they would play some more. Once Sydney learned to associate the smell of marijuana with her favorite toy, Dani was able to hide drugs and have Sydney sniff them out. Anytime she found them, she was rewarded with a game of tug of war.

"Some over here too," Aaron hollered from the kitchen.

Dani ended the tug-of-war game, handed her brick to another officer, and sent Sydney off again. Another brick was stashed under the bed and a fourth under the bathroom sink.

When the house was cleared, there was quite the stash accrued.

"Do we know where the owner is?" Dani asked Lieutenant Craig when the search was complete.

"On the run, we assume. We'll have to return to the precinct and check the database to see if we can find family or friends who might have an idea of his whereabouts."

"It seems odd he would leave without the drugs, doesn't it?" Dani pressed.

"It does, but we don't have the full picture of what happened at that warehouse. If Chris wasn't killed, whoever killed the man we found might be after him. All we know is that he was there. Either way, we'll keep looking."

3

Calvin sighed with relief when the knock at the door sounded. He had been up all night worrying about Chris. Yes, his brother needed tough love, but Calvin couldn't shake the feeling that Chris might be in real trouble this time. His brown eyes had held a sadness, but as Calvin thought more about it, he wondered if they also held fear.

His relief was short lived though when he opened the door and found not Calvin but three police officers and two German shepherds.

"Calvin Phillips?"

"Yes, I'm Calvin." What kind of trouble was Chris in?

"I'm Lieutenant Craig, and this is officer Jones and Higgins. We're looking for your brother, Chris Phillips."

"He's not here," Calvin said, but as he spoke the two German shepherds tugged on their leashes, straining to enter the room.

"The dogs say otherwise. Do you mind if we look around?" Lieutenant Craig asked.

Calvin would have allowed them in even if the man hadn't resembled Arnold Schwarzenegger. He backed against the wall, allowing the officers and K-9 dogs into his apartment.

The dogs made a beeline for his couch, and after a moment of sniffing, one pulled a mitten triumphantly from the couch cushions.

As the officer, a trim blonde turned her hazel eyes on him, Calvin spoke up. "Chris was here yesterday. He must have dropped the mitten when we were watching the game, but I swear to you he's not here now."

"Do you know where he might be?" Lieutenant Craig asked. With his close-cut hair and steely gaze, Calvin wondered if he were ex-marine.

"I thought he went home to his place when he left here." He glanced around at the dogs and the other two officers searching the rest of his place. "Is he in trouble?"

The lieutenant's eyebrow arched. "He didn't tell you?"

Calvin shook his head. "I didn't let him. He came

here yesterday looking for money, but I didn't give him any. We watched the game, and then he left."

"Your brother is a person of interest in a homicide case."

Calvin's jaw dropped as his eyes widened. "Homicide? No way, not Chris. He's made some mistakes, but he's no killer."

"If he's not responsible for the murder," Lieutenant Craig said, "then it's very likely some bad men are looking for him. We can definitely place your brother at the scene. It would be in his best interest for you to tell us of any place he might hide."

Calvin could think of only one place, but he couldn't give the information to the police. He needed to check it out first and hear Chris's side of the story. What kind of trouble had he gotten himself into now?

"He works overnights at the Walmart in Lacey. It's possible he's staying with a co-worker if he's not at his house, but I don't know who he hangs out with there."

"That's fine. We can check. Thank you for your cooperation, Mr. Phillips."

"House is clear, Lieutenant," the male K-9 officer said as the two reappeared in the living room. He was much older than his female partner with salt and pepper hair and leathery skin.

"If you see him, here's my card," the lieutenant

said, holding out a white business card. "You should call."

Calvin took the card and nodded. He politely ushered the cops to the door, but as soon as the door closed behind them, he turned the lock and headed for the hall closet. After a little digging, he found his duffle bag and hurried to the bedroom to pack.

After tossing the bag on the bed, he flicked on the television to check the local weather. A storm was coming, and he needed to know how much time remained before the snow arrived and increased the chances of getting stranded in the cabin for a few days.

"The storm is expected to hit late tonight with the heaviest snow hitting the Cascade foothills. Five to seven inches of snow is predicted in the foothills with one to three inches in the surrounding areas closer to the sound."

Though the woman continued, Calvin stopped listening. If five to seven inches were expected tonight, he better plan to be there for a few days. Sometimes the cabin didn't get as much snow as predicted, but as it lay near Evergreen ridge in a heavily wooded area, it sometimes suffered from "silver thaws." These were dangerous ice storms that sometimes caused tree branches to fall and block the roads.

After packing his clothes and toiletries, he powered up his laptop to send a message to his employer.

Calvin had enough vacation days saved up he could afford to take a few days off. He just hoped it wouldn't be any longer than that. He tapped out the email, hit send, and then grabbed the bags.

Calvin was about to start the truck when he realized he would need food. He hadn't been at the cabin in ages and he had no idea what might be there. After locking the truck, he hurried back inside to grab some food from the fridge along with a few canned items. With haste, he tossed them into another bag and returned to the truck.

"Lord, please let me get there before the snow," he prayed as he shoved the key in the ignition and turned. The truck roared to life and Calvin backed it out of the space. He just needed four hours.

4

"How does that happen?" Dani asked Aaron as they loaded into the SUV.

"What?" Aaron asked as he started the rig.

"How does one brother go so wrong and the other appear stable?"

"Yeah, that's a good question, but I don't have an answer," he replied.

"Do you think he was hiding something?" Dani asked, switching the subject.

"We searched the house, DP. We didn't find anything else."

"I know, but there was this moment when the lieutenant asked if he knew where Chris was, I noticed him tense. Like he had an idea but didn't want to share it."

Aaron glanced away from the road long enough to

flash her an incredulous look. "You've been watching too much Criminal Minds, DP."

"Maybe," Dani said, but she knew what she had seen.

Her attention to detail was one of the things that made her a great cop. Having always loved puzzles, she excelled at the kind where you looked at a scene and then when something moved or disappeared you figured out what. Aaron was more old school.

He wasn't a bad cop, and Dani would never do anything to propagate stereotypes, but if cops really did sit in donut shops, she always felt Aaron would be the one. He enjoyed his coffee and breakfast every morning, and while top-notch when at work, Dani knew he didn't take work home with him. But he had a wife and kids, and Dani had…. Sydney.

Dani wanted more: the husband, the house, the two point five kids - she already owned the dog. But she was picky. After watching her own mother marry and divorce three times, Dani didn't want to go through that. She wanted her marriage to be right, to be to "the one" if such a thing existed. She thought she had found it with James, but shortly after he proposed, she found out he was also dating his secretary. And so, even though she was nearing twenty-seven, she remained single.

When they returned to the station, Dani gathered

her stuff, said goodnight to Aaron, and headed home with Sydney.

Her dark, quiet house greeted her. She favored the quiet most days as it allowed her to think, but every once in a while, the quiet pressed down on her. Those were the times she wished she had someone to come home to, to share her day with. Someone who could talk, unlike her furry companion. James had carried on conversations, but everything else had been a lie, and she'd rather be alone than live a lie.

"What do you think, Sydney?" she asked, petting the dog's head. "Am I wrong? Or was Calvin hiding something?"

Sydney simply stared at her with soulful brown eyes.

Dani sighed. "Yeah, maybe you're right. Maybe I'm reading too much into it." She reached up to the cabinet and pulled out a treat for Sydney.

With a careful bite, the dog grabbed the treat and took it to her favorite spot beside the faded leather couch. Dani poured herself a glass of red wine and brought it into the living room as well.

She turned on the television and curled up under a blanket, but she couldn't focus on the show. Instead, she kept replaying the scene over and over in her head. Something just didn't sit right with her, but it wasn't her case any longer. She needed to just let it go.

5

C alvin pulled up to the cabin just as the first flakes of snow began to fall. He saw no other car, but Chris might have hitched a ride or taken the bus. The nearest stop lay a few miles away, but he could have walked the distance. Calvin parked the truck in front and grabbed his bags.

The front porch creaked and groaned under his weight, and Calvin made a mental note to fix it soon. He couldn't remember the last time he visited the cabin, definitely some time ago. Lots of little repairs probably needed to be done.

He tried the knob, but the front door was locked. After flipping through his keys, he secured the right one and unlocked the door. It opened with a stiff creak, and a musty odor wafted out.

"Chris?" Calvin hollered as he stepped inside. Only

silence returned his greeting. So, he wasn't here. Or perhaps he was out getting firewood. The cold would definitely set in tonight.

Calvin shut the door behind him and placed his bag of clothes down on the couch. A few logs lay near the fireplace, enough to provide heat through the night, but he would need to gather more in the morning when the sun provided more light.

He wandered into the kitchen, but no sign of Chris existed there. A layer of dust coated the counter and the small wooden table. Calvin set the bag with the food down on the table before turning to the hallway to check the bedrooms. The cabin contained only two - a master bedroom his parents had shared and the smaller second one he and Chris roomed in when staying here.

The master lay on the left, and Calvin pushed open the door. A wave of nostalgia hit him as a memory from one family adventure washed over him.

"What are you doing out of bed, Calvin?" his mother asked. She wore a red and black flannel shirt and a ski cap. The heat hadn't filtered throughout the cabin yet, and the air held a chill.

"I'm cold, Mom. Can I sleep with you? For a little bit?"

Her kind smile reached her eyes, and she patted the bed next to her. "Sure, but only till it warms up."

Calvin charged into the room and climbed in bed next to

his mother, snuggling into her side. She smelled of campfire and cookies, and as he closed his eyes, he couldn't remember a nicer smell.

Calvin chuckled at the memory. The heat never filled the room that night and the four of them ended up in his parent's bed together. Though a tight squeeze, Calvin couldn't remember a happier time.

No sign of Chris appeared in this room either though. The faded flowered comforter appeared untouched and a similar coating of dust lay on the small dresser in the room. With a sigh, Calvin backed from the room and closed the door.

He turned and opened the other room, but it too lay empty. Just the queen bed he and Chris had shared and a small dresser and lamp.

So, Chris hadn't been here. Had Calvin been wrong? Or perhaps Chris just hadn't arrived yet. He decided to wait a day or so and see if Chris showed up. Calvin knew of nowhere else Chris would go, and he could wait.

He made his way back into the living room and piled up some logs in the fireplace to start a fire. It took a few matches, but after a few minutes, a gentle warmth emanated from the area.

With that taken care of, he decided to scrounge up some dinner. He unloaded the food he had brought first, but as he opened the fridge, he realized no electricity powered it. The snow must have knocked out a power line. He'd have to improvise. After a little bit of digging, he found an old cooler under a cabinet. He loaded the cooler with snow from the back porch and placed the eggs and milk inside.

The canned foods he added to the cupboards which weren't stocked but did yield a few cans of chili and corn. He wiped off the counters with a few paper towels and then rummaged in the drawers until he found a can opener and a spoon. Another bit of searching yielded him a few pots and a couple of bowls. The stove was a gas stove, a small miracle, and the burner flamed to life with the help of another match.

As he sat down at the table with his dinner, he pulled out his phone and made a list of supplies he should get to restock the cabin. Then he turned the phone off. If there was no electricity, he didn't want to run his battery down in case he needed it. Hopefully, Chris would show up soon and they could head back in the morning.

The snow continued to fall outside, and as Calvin watched the gentle flakes, he realized he had forgotten the peace this place exuded. His life wasn't super hectic with his work from home job, but even so, it would be nice to come out here some days and just unplug. No laptop, no phone, no stress.

Well, other than his worry over Chris. "Lord," he said looking up at the ceiling as if he could see God staring down at him from heaven. "I don't know what trouble Chris is in this time, but please protect him. Keep him safe with whatever's going on. He needs your help. We only have each other left. Help me find him before the police do. Amen."

He wasn't sure when he began praying looking up at God instead of closing his eyes - maybe after his parent's deaths when he felt he needed more consolation, but he found he liked it now. It made it feel as if God were in the room with him.

When the chili and corn were gone, Calvin washed the pots and the bowls in the sink and set them in the dish rack to dry. Thankfully, the water was provided from the nearby town and not from a well, so the lack of electricity didn't affect it. Calvin glanced out the window as he wiped his hands on a nearby towel. The outside was now completely white and the snow was falling much harder than when he had arrived. Big fat flakes fell one after the other in a steady stream of white.

As he shivered, he realized the temperature inside had dropped as well. He hadn't noticed it while eating as the warmth from the stove had heated the kitchen for a bit, but now the cold seeped in with icy talons and scraped across his skin.

He threw another few logs on the fire and wrapped the blanket from the back of the couch around him. As he watched the flames dance to and fro, he wondered if this cabin would ever see the happiness of a family again. Would he find a wife and bring her and his children here? Would Chris?

Calvin hadn't thought he was ready for love again but coming here reminded him how nice it was to have family - how happy his parents had been. Maybe, if he could get Chris's life back on track, he could focus on his own.

6

D ani trudged through the snow in the parking lot, muttering under her breath. She hated snow, and she hated being cold. Thankfully, Olympia didn't often get snow, but when it did, everything slowed down. No one knew how to drive in it, and there weren't enough snow plows to keep the roads as clear as she would like.

Sydney never seemed to mind though, and while she was a police dog, she still liked to play in the white powder and had stared longingly out Dani's back door once the flakes began to fall.

Dani hadn't let her outside, but now Sydney strutted proudly through the few inches as if to declare her enjoyment.

"Don't bother unpacking," Aaron said as he met her at the door. "We found out Chris's family owns a cabin near the gorge. The lieutenant has ordered us out there to search for signs of him."

"Can I at least get some coffee?" Dani asked. She had been up too late last night running things through her mind.

"On the way," he said.

With a sigh that sent her slender shoulders heaving, Dani turned around and followed him back out into the cold. "I told you he was hiding something," she said. "Why wouldn't he tell us about the cabin?"

"Who?" Aaron asked as he pressed the key fob button to open the back door of the SUV.

"The guy from yesterday. The brother. I told you he was hiding something."

"Maybe he forgot," Aaron said, strapping his dog in place. "Or perhaps he didn't know."

"He didn't know his family had a cabin a few hours from here?" Dani asked with a raised eyebrow. "Now who's tossing out conspiracy theories? Do you think he's in on it then?"

"I guess we'll find out when we get there, DP. Come on, load up."

Dani secured Sydney next to Dexter and climbed into the passenger seat. "Don't forget, you said we could get coffee," she said as a shiver ran down her spine.

"You know if you dressed warmer when it snowed,

you might not need so much coffee," Aaron said as he started the engine.

Dani looked down at her outfit. She had on her black BDU pants and shirt. "What do you mean? I'm in uniform."

"Yeah, but I bet you don't have layers underneath. You can wear thermals under your uniform when it's cold out."

Dani scrunched her nose in disgust. "But then I'd be all bulky and hot when inside."

Aaron shrugged. "At least you wouldn't freeze."

"I grew up in Texas," she said. "We had like three snows my whole life and we didn't dress in layers because a day later it was all gone." She shot him a look as she pushed the button to turn on the heated seats. Modern conveniences were made so she wouldn't have to suffer through the cold.

With the coffee stop and a bathroom break, it took them just over four hours to get to Evergreen Ridge. The snow was thicker out here, and Dani wished she had worn insulated boots at least. She hoped this would be a quick excursion.

"Crap. We'll have to walk in," Aaron said, pulling the SUV over to the side of the road.

"What?" Dani asked. She hadn't expected to be tromping through the snow.

"Yeah, the snow's too high here. The SUV won't

make it through. Don't worry though. The GPS says we're only about a mile from the cabin."

Dani's jaw dropped, and she blinked at him. "A mile? I didn't dress to walk a mile in the snow."

Aaron smiled at her. "Well, then I guess you will next time." His tone softened as he spoke again, "Look, I wasn't expecting this much snow either, but at least our boots are waterproof. We'll get in, look around, and then get back here. No big deal."

She narrowed her eyes and shot him a glare as she climbed out of the car. The snow was up to the middle of her calves, and she immediately felt the cold seep into her legs. "Let's get this done," she said as she reached the back and unhooked Sydney.

The dogs jumped down and pranced in the snow, sending flurries of white into the air.

"This way," Aaron said after locking the SUV.

Dani followed him, trudging through the thick snow. Not only would she be frozen after this, but she'd be all sweaty. It was hard work moving her small frame through the drifts without snowshoes.

As they walked, the trees grew closer to them, crowding in and creating a quiet serenity.

"You have to admit," Aaron said, checking the GPS again, "you can't beat the scenery."

"I guess," Dani replied. She was actually enjoying

the quiet peacefulness, but he didn't need to know that.

The further they walked into the forest, the darker it became. Dani glanced up to see where the sun had gone, but it was obscured by the thick branches covered in snow. Some of them were bowing under the weight of the white powder.

"Um, Aaron, do you think it's safe walking under all these trees?" she asked. Her question was punctuated by a creaking sound, a crack, and then a branch falling off to the right.

"It's fine," he said, "just keep your eyes open and pay attention to the sounds."

Dani nodded, but the easy, peaceful feeling was gone. With every creak and groan around her, she glanced wildly up at the tall trees that now looked like menacing giants encircling them.

"Looks like only another quarter mile to go," Aaron said.

Dani shivered, both from the cold and from the eerie feeling that had blanketed her. Suddenly, a loud crack sounded. Dani's gaze shot up, but her feet froze. A large limb was hurtling down toward her.

"DP, move," Aaron shouted, but her feet wouldn't obey.

Dani threw her hands up to shield herself and closed her eyes. Pain like she had never felt seared through her, knocking her to the ground and stealing her breath.

"DP." Aaron's worried voice carried over to her.

Dani opened her eyes and blinked a few times to try to get rid of the stars blurring her vision. Sydney's nose touched her face and then Aaron's concerned face came into view.

"Are you okay?" he asked.

"I'm not sure," she wheezed. Every breath hurt. "I think I broke a rib."

His eyes scanned from her head to her toe. "Anywhere else?"

"My back," she said. "And I'm cold." The snow was piled up around her and quickly sinking in through her BDUs.

Aaron pushed against the large branch pinning her down, but it didn't budge. He tried squatting and lifting, but that did nothing either. "It's too heavy. I'm going to have to go get some help." He shrugged off his coat and pushed it against her. "Try to stay warm. I'll be back with help as soon as I can."

Dani's teeth chattered, but she tried to clench them together to keep Aaron from worrying. "I'm not going anywhere," she joked and then cringed at the pain.

Worry clouded Aaron's eyes and she knew he was assessing to see if there were another option, but there was none. Him returning to the closest town to get help was their best option.

"Okay," he said finally. "I'll be back. Stay with her Sydney."

Sydney looked up at him and then replaced her nose in the crook of Dani's shoulder. As Aaron walked away, Dani tried to think happy, calming, warm thoughts. But the truth was, it was cold out here and if Aaron didn't get back quickly, she would become hypothermic.

7

Calvin was just about to fire up the chain saw when a German shepherd bolted into view. The black K-9 band around its chest grabbed his attention. Was this one of the dogs from his house visit yesterday?

The dog sat at his feet and looked up at him. "What is it? Where's your officer?" The dog stared at him a moment longer and then gently bit his pant leg and began backing up. "Do you want me to follow you?" Calvin asked.

He had only been joking, but the dog wagged its tail and then turned toward the deeper part of the forest. Calvin followed, not sure where the dog was leading him, but curious all the same. His curiosity quickly morphed into fear when he saw the female officer from the day before pinned beneath a large tree branch. Though a jacket was shoved up against her, her lips were blue, and her eyes were closed. Calvin was glad he hadn't left the chainsaw back at the clearing though he had no idea why he hadn't.

Calvin bent down and checked for a pulse. There, but just barely. He needed to get her out of the cold and warmed up. Though not an EMT, he knew moving a victim was not the best idea. However, with the surrounding elements, Calvin had little choice. He fired up the chain saw and began cutting as close to the woman as he could while still making sure he didn't hit her. The dog sat watching a few feet away.

After a minute, he freed one side of the large limb. Calvin pushed the piece of wood off the woman and glanced around. He didn't have anything to carry her back with, and he wanted to move her as little as possible. He wished he'd brought the sled with him that he planned to load the firewood on. Unfortunately, it still sat in the clearing, and now he wasn't sure he should take the time to go get it.

A few feet away, lay a large leafy branch. If he could strap her to it with the jacket, maybe he could pull her back to the cabin. It took a few minutes of scuffling to get the branch situated behind her. He squatted, hooking his arms under hers and walked backwards, pulling her onto the branch. As carefully as possible, he tied the jacket around her hips and the branch to help secure her. Though it would probably have been more secure if he had tied it higher, he feared her ribs were injured from the fallen limb and he didn't want to make it any worse.

"Okay, dog," he said to the K-9. "Let's get out of the cold, shall we?"

The trip back to the cabin was long and arduous, but Calvin finally reached the front door. He whispered a silent prayer of thanks for the snow that covered the steps enough to make a ramp he could hoist the woman up. Once inside, he maneuvered her near the fireplace where the last of the logs burned. The dog sat down at her side.

"I have to get more firewood, but I'll be back." Calvin shook his head as he realized he was talking to the dog as if it were a person. Or maybe he hoped the woman would be able to hear him.

After a final glance at her - she still hadn't moved - he exited the cabin and picked up the chain saw from the porch where he had dropped it. With a hastened step, he returned to the grove of trees he had been in when the dog found him. After firing up the chain saw again, he cut down one and made short work of the wood, placing it on the sled he had originally brought with him this morning and forgotten when the dog showed up.

Calvin stacked the new wood against the side of the

cabin and stepped back, regarding the pile. It should be enough to last another few days, and he hoped to be home after that.

Now, it was time to scour the ground for some dead wood for the fire. The freshly cut wood would smoke like mad if he could even get it lit, but if he could find a few good pieces that were dry inside, he should be okay.

The pickings were slim, but he managed to find an armful he thought would burn well and brought it inside where the woman still lay on the floor. After stacking it up beside the fireplace, he sat down on the couch and waited. The woman's skin was no longer pale, her lips no longer blue. His gut told him she would be stirring soon, but he wanted to take no chances. He turned his face upward and began praying for the safety of the woman.

8

Dani's eyes felt heavy and glued shut. A forced effort opened them, and she looked around. The first thing she noticed was the lack of cold. In fact, a small fire burned from a fireplace a few feet away, warming her. The realization no snow surrounded her came next. She was no longer out in the elements, but inside. The question was - inside where? Had Aaron come back for her already?

Sydney's wet nose poked her cheek, and instinctively she reached her hand up to pet the dog, but a searing pain through her chest stopped the movement.

"Ugh," she groaned.

"Where does it hurt?" The voice was not one she recognized, but a moment later, a slightly familiar face appeared in her vision. The man from the previous day.

"You," she wheezed. "Where's your brother?"

"Not here," the man said with a shake of his head. "But really is that your biggest concern in your condition?"

"I'm fine," Dani said and grimaced as the pain pounded again. She didn't know this man, but she hated that he was seeing her in this condition. Dani learned long ago as a woman in a male-dominated career, she needed to be tough, even when she felt like death. It was one reason she opted to shorten her name to the more masculine form.

"Yes, I can see that," he said, a smile tugging at his lips. "Still, we should check you out to determine the extent of your injuries. I don't want to move you any more until we determine there won't be lasting damage."

"What are you, a doctor?" Dani asked.

"No, but I interned with EMTs one summer. I don't know much, but I'm all you've got right now."

"My partner will be back soon, so you better not think of trying anything," Dani said. She hated that the pain kept her from standing and arresting him herself.

"I'm not your enemy," the man said and ran a hand through his brown hair. A woody, smoky scent drifted to Dani's face. "Look, why don't we start over. I'm Calvin, and you are?"

Dani paused, weighing her options. She was basically at the mercy of this man until she healed. In her current condition, she could barely move. There was no way she could give chase and apprehend a suspect. Besides, her gut told her he wasn't involved in whatever his brother was, and she had learned to trust it a long time ago. "Dani," she replied.

"Okay, Dani, I'm almost positive your ribs are bruised if not broken since the tree was across them, but do you hurt anywhere else?"

Dani performed a mental analysis of her body. Her head throbbed slightly but probably only from the fall. She could wiggle her toes, so she didn't believe she had injured her back. "No, I think it's just my ribs. I imagine I'll be sore, but I can probably sit up if you can help me."

Calvin bit his bottom lip and his brow furrowed, but he reached out a hand. "Okay, if you're sure, but let's take it slow."

As his arm slipped under her neck, a tiny jolt of electricity shot through Dani. Her eyes flicked up to his, and from his widened gaze, she believed he felt it too. She didn't have time to think about it long though as the pain increased as soon as she moved. Darkness clouded her vision, and she forced her eyes shut to try to combat the wave of nausea erupting in her stomach.

With slow steps, they made their way to the couch and Calvin helped her lie down. Dani tried to control her breathing as every breath hurt and the short walk left her winded. "Thank you," she said, holding her chest.

"Let me get you some ice and see if I have any Tylenol," Calvin said and hurried into the kitchen area. He searched for the pain medicine first, finding an old bottle in one of the cabinets. The ice pack, however, proved to be trickier.

Though one resided in the freezer, it was only slightly cool now due to the lack of electricity. After a little more rummaging, Calvin found a ziplock bag big enough to hold the ice pack. He shoved the pack in and then opened the back door, scooping up more snow and filling the bag around the pack. It wasn't perfect, but hopefully it would help. With the bag in one hand and the bottle in the other, he returned to the living room.

Dani took the bottle first, opened the lid and shook out two pills which she downed without a drop of water. Then she took the pack with a slight smile and placed it on her ribs. "How come you didn't become an EMT? You seem good at it."

Calvin's face fell, and he rubbed a hand across his chin. "I wanted to, and uh, then my dad got sick. I took some time off to help my mom with him. He was a fighter, but the cancer got him in the end."

Dani's heart ached at the pain etched in Calvin's face. It was clear he had cared greatly for his father.

"After that, I went back to it, but it was harder. I kept thinking I should have been able to save him, you know? Then, my mom was killed in a car accident a few months later. I wasn't on shift, and I couldn't have done anything even if I had been, but I couldn't stay in it. Just didn't have the heart anymore. Plus, Chris was still in college, and I needed a better paying job to help him out, so I fell back on computer programming. It paid well, and I didn't have to be around people."

"Is that when Chris turned to drugs?"

Calvin sighed. "Yeah, I turned to work, and he turned to drugs. He's no killer, though."

"You should have told us about the cabin, Calvin."

"I understand," he said, "but I wanted to hear Chris's side myself. He's my brother, you know?"

Dani didn't really know what that was like. She had been an only child until about the age of six when her mother first remarried. Then her half-sister, Gabby, had been born. A few years later, Dani's mother had divorced Gabby's father and married Ray. She'd had twin boys with him, Derek and Eric. The next year, they had divorced. So, while Dani had siblings, she wasn't especially close to any of them, as they often spent time with their fathers and apart from her. Gabby was probably her closest sibling and that had more to do with their shared gender than anything else.

"So, he hasn't been here?" she asked, avoiding his question.

He shook his head. "No, I thought he might come here, but there was no sign of him when I arrived. I planned to give him a few days to see if he showed up."

"If my partner doesn't find us first, we should head out tomorrow to find him. We can have someone watch the cabin in case your brother shows up."

Calvin raised his brow at her. "I doubt we're going anywhere tomorrow. Didn't you see the snow out there?"

"Yes, but my partner won't know where I've gone. I can't just disappear."

"Your partner might not even be able to get back. There's another storm expected tonight, and it will probably close the road in."

Dani's eyes widened. "You mean I'm stuck here?"

Calvin laughed. It was a deep timbre sound. "You don't have to make it sound so awful. You need time to heal anyway. Though from what I remember, you shouldn't spend too much time lying down. I seem to remember the suggestion was to try to continue normal activity and take as deep of breaths as you can so that fluid doesn't build up in your lungs."

Dani blinked as her mind raced through options. Her radio had been broken when the tree fell on her, and she had left her cell in the SUV. "Phone. Do you at least have a phone, so I can call and let someone know I'm okay?"

"Sorry," he said with a shrug. "No service right now. I think the storm knocked down some power lines. It's why we don't have electricity either."

"Smoke signal?" Dani asked, but she was only half kidding. If Aaron came back and found her gone, surely, he would continue to the cabin. But what if he was caught in the snow? What if he never made it back to the closest town? Or what if he did and couldn't get back to her? Was she going to be stuck with this man she didn't know for days? She had no change of clothes, no toiletries.

"How about I make us some dinner?" Calvin offered, breaking into her runaway thoughts.

Dani nodded absentmindedly. She wasn't really hungry though she knew she needed to eat to keep her strength.

As Calvin turned into the kitchen, Sydney laid her head on Dani's lap.

"It'll be okay, girl," Dani said, stroking the top of Sydney's head. "We'll figure something out."

9

"Can you make it to the table to eat?" Calvin asked Dani when the dinner was ready. It wasn't much, just hot dogs and canned beans. He wished he had brought better food, but in his hurry to find Chris, he had simply grabbed what was in his fridge.

"Yeah, I think I can," she said, though the grimace that crossed her face said otherwise.

Calvin leaned down and snaked an arm around Dani's waist. As he did, the intoxicating flowery scent of her perfume or shampoo filled his nose. His eyes flicked to hers, and his heart sped up as he realized her face resided only inches from his. From here, the tiny flecks of gold and green popped in her hazel eyes. He dropped his eyes for a moment as the intense urge to kiss her filled him.

"Easy," he said as she groaned and pinched lines of pain etched across her face.

"I'm okay," she wheezed.

Once upright, breathing became easier for Dani. Easier, but not perfect. Her breaths still came in shallow gasps. When she dropped her arm from his waist, he followed suit though he didn't want to. How long had it been since he had held a woman in his arms?

There had been no one serious since his parents' death. He had dated a few women he had met at church, but every time he felt himself getting close, he would pull away. Too much pain still remained in his heart.

After Dani was situated at the table, Calvin brought the plates of food. "Sorry it's not more," he said, "but I wasn't expecting company."

"It's fine," Dani said. "I'll eat just about anything when I'm hungry."

Calvin bowed his head as she picked up her hotdog. He had once felt awkward praying in front of people, even when he prayed in his head and they couldn't hear him, but the last few years, prayer had been all that had kept him going.

"You still pray?" Dani asked him when he opened his eyes.

"What do you mean?" he asked.

"I mean after your parents dying and your brother turning to drugs, how can you still believe in a God?"

Calvin took a deep breath as he debated his next words. "When my dad first got sick, I thought like that. Why would a loving God take my dad when he was still so young? I did a lot of soul-searching and talked to a lot of pastors. The conclusion I came to was this: I'm not God, and I don't have all the answers, but I believe He knows what He's doing.

"See, I don't believe this is the end. I believe there will be a better place after this in Heaven. My dad was a Christian, and if I truly trust in God, which I do, then I know my father is in a better place. Why did he get cancer? I don't have that answer. Why was my mother killed so soon after? I don't know that either. But either I take solace in the one thing I do know - that God is in control - or I go crazy and lose my faith in everything."

Dani blinked at him, but it was impossible to read what she was thinking. "I guess I never thought of it like that," she said.

"Are you a believer?" Calvin asked. He found himself holding his breath as he awaited her answer. Though he didn't want to be attracted to her, he couldn't deny the pull he was feeling.

"I mean I guess I believe in something," she said, "but the last time I went to church, it didn't turn out so well."

Calvin's heart plummeted, but she hadn't flat out said no which meant there was hope. He would pray for her and continue to talk with her if she was open, but not now. Now, he wanted to know more about her.

"What made you become a K-9 officer?" he asked before taking a bite of his own hotdog.

Dani glanced down at the German shepherd who lay at their feet. "I always wanted a pet growing up, but my mom was more interested in raising husbands than dogs, so we never got to have one. When I joined the academy, I knew I wanted to be more than a beat cop. I mean, don't get me wrong, it's a great place to start and some people love it so much they never leave, but I wanted something different. So, when a slot at the K-9 academy opened up, I jumped on it. Sydney and I just recently graduated. In fact, your brother was our first case."

She paused and flashed him a tight smile. "Sorry, I didn't mean for that to sound so excited."

"It's okay," he said. "It's nice that you are so committed and enjoy your job. Besides, while I love my brother, he has made some pretty big mistakes. I just hope I can help get him on the right path before it's too late."

The conversation stalled after that and they finished eating in silence. When his plate was empty, Calvin stood and began gathering the dishes to wash.

"There's one more hotdog in the pan. Can I give it to your dog?"

"She would love that," Dani said. "It's not her normal fare, but I guess she'll survive one night."

Calvin smiled and cut up the hotdog, but he wondered if it would be just one night. The snow had gotten thick, too thick for him to drive out. He could probably walk the mile to the road in hopes of finding someone to help, but he wasn't sure Dani could in her condition. She hadn't said a word about the pain, but he could see the grimace of pain every time she moved or took too deep a breath.

He placed the cut-up wiener on the floor for the dog and then finished the dishes.

"Would you like to play a game?" he asked Dani as he hung the towel over the rack to dry. "I could fire up a lantern and we could dust off one of the old board games." The sun had quickly lowered position in the sky and only a faint beam of light sneaked in the windows.

"Do you have Scrabble?" she asked, her eyes lighting up. "I always loved Scrabble."

"Well now, what cabin in the woods would be complete without a Scrabble board?" he teased. Calvin retrieved the game from the hall shelf and placed it on the table for her to set up while he lit a lantern.

"Did you play Scrabble often?" she asked when he

re-joined her. The board was set up and all the tiles were laid face down.

"My mom and I did," he answered, thinking back. "But Chris and my dad were usually off playing in the woods or fishing."

"You didn't like fishing?" she asked with a teasing twinkle in her eye.

Calvin chuckled. "To be honest, I found it boring. I generally preferred reading or building a computer program."

"What's your favorite book?" She flipped over a tile revealing a one point "I" and frowned.

Calvin flipped over the ten-point J and smiled.

"Cheater," she said as she swirled the tiles around.

"I guess my favorite book was *The Princess Bride*," he said as he picked up his seven tiles to start with.

"No way," she said.

"Yes way, you do know it was a book as well, right?"

"Yes, I know it was a book," she said, wrinkling her brow at him. "It was my favorite book too."

He stared at her unsure if she were serious or jerking his chain.

"I mean the movie was great, but the book was even better. Though I have to admit, I found myself saying 'inconceivable' just like the actor as I read the book again after watching the movie."

"Me too," he said and for a moment they shared a look.

Then she broke the connection. "I should warn you, I kick tail at Scrabble."

"Hah, you can try." With a flourish, he laid the word 'jumped' down on the Scrabble board. "Hmm, twenty-three points with a double word score makes that," he paused as he pretended to count, "forty-six."

"That's pretty good," she said, "but the game is just beginning."

Calvin smiled as Dani scrutinized her tiles. Her lips twisted into a funny shape and lines broke out on her forehead as she thought, but Calvin still found her attractive. In fact, he found his attention drawn to her lips. What would they feel like? Taste like?

Her blonde hair just brushed her shoulders and Calvin wondered how it would feel against his hand.

"Hey, earth to Calvin." Dani waved a hand in front of his face. "It's your turn."

"Right, sorry." With great effort, he pushed thoughts of Dani's lips from his mind and focused on his letters.

10

Dani regarded Calvin as he concentrated on his tiles. He was quite handsome though she wasn't sure about the beard. She'd never kissed a man with a beard before, and she wasn't sure if she would enjoy the experience. Would it be soft or rough like sandpaper?

"There," he announced proudly as he lay all but one tile down. "Fourteen more points brings my total to two hundred ninety-seven."

Dani smiled as she looked at her letters. He had left the space she needed open, and she plopped down all her remaining letters spelling larynx and fifty-one points.

"So that brings my total to three hundred thirty-two compared to your two hundred ninety-seven," she said smugly. "I told you I kicked tail."

"This time," he said, "but I demand a rematch."

"Tomorrow," Dani said, stifling a yawn. "I was up too early today."

"I'll hold you to that," he said with a smile.

Dani smiled back, and a blush colored her cheeks as she pictured him holding her. She shook her head. What was she thinking? She still wasn't sure he was completely innocent and even if he was, she would have to bring his brother in. That didn't make for a stellar start to a relationship.

Calvin cleared his throat. "So, um, there's the master bedroom where my parents always slept. There's the guest room where Chris and I bunked, or there's the couch. I slept on it last night. It's not the most comfortable, but it's probably the warmest. Do you have a preference?"

Dani bit back a grin as a flash of red colored his cheeks and his eyes dropped to the floor. "Um, I guess I can take the master bedroom, but uh… do you have an oversized shirt or something I can borrow? I didn't really plan on being stranded and this uniform isn't the most comfortable to sleep in."

"Oh, um, let me check," Calvin said as another wave of red flooded his face. He disappeared down the hall for a moment and then returned with a faded black Toby Mac t-shirt. It appeared very worn and comfortable and would be way better than her uniform.

"You go on the run and that is what you bring?" Dani asked in a teasing voice.

He shrugged. "I grabbed what was closest. This is my favorite shirt by the way. Have you ever seen him in concert?"

"No, but I have heard his songs on the radio. While I'm not much for Christian music, he is pretty good, and thank you," Dani said, taking the shirt. "I don't suppose you have an extra toothbrush or toothpaste at least?" It was a stretch and she knew it, but she hated going to bed with unbrushed teeth. She always woke in the middle of the night when she didn't brush and hated the scuzzy feeling on them.

"No extra brush," he said slowly, "but I'll happily share my toothpaste."

Toothpaste was better than nothing, so Dani agreed. She followed him down the hallway and to the master bedroom.

"There you go," he said, pointing in the room. "Feel free to look around and see if you find anything else you need or can use. I'll be across the hall here." He looked to the door across the hall. "The bathroom is that door there."

"Thank you," Dani said. "Is it alright if Sydney

sleeps in here with me? She's used to being by my side at home."

"Of course," he said. "Whatever you need."

"Come here, girl," Dani called to the German shepherd who padded into the room, sniffed around a bit, and curled up at the foot of the bed. "Well, I guess she thinks it's okay," Dani said with a smile.

"I'll leave the toothpaste on the sink for you," Calvin said. "Sleep well."

Dani didn't think much hope resided in that. Not only was she not in her house, but she didn't have her favorite sleepwear - a pair of shorts and a soft purple cotton tee. She also didn't have her toothbrush or her pillows. Gabby had often teased her growing up about her need for multiple pillows, but Dani had never minded. As long as she got a good sleep, she didn't care if she got teased.

And of course, there were her ribs. Broken or bruised, she wasn't sure, but the amount of pain suggested broken. Regardless, the pain would more than likely keep her awake.

Dani unbuttoned and slipped off her BDU shirt, grunting slightly from the additional pain. Then she slipped on Calvin's tee. A masculine woodsy smell drifted up from the shirt and Dani inhaled. How long had it been since her last boyfriend? Before K-9 school, that was for sure.

The shirt fell below her butt, but it wasn't quite long enough for Dani's modesty, so she turned her attention to the dresser. She had no idea if Calvin's mother had left any clothes here or even what size she had been, but it was either something of hers or nothing under her shirt. Dani would never be able to sleep comfortably in her BDU pants.

The first drawer revealed a few sweaters, mittens, and a hat. The second held a pair of pants and a long sleeve shirt. In the third drawer, she struck gold. A soft pink pair of pajama pants sporting a flower design stared up at her. They were hideously out of date and definitely not her style, but Dani couldn't care less as long as they fit.

The pants were a little big and therefore sat more on her hip bones than her waist, but they had a draw-string and they would work. After a final check to make sure she was covered, Dani opened the door and shuffled down the hallway to the bathroom.

True to his word, Calvin had left a tube of tooth-paste on the sink. Crest Whitening - her favorite. She squeezed some onto her finger after washing it and then placed the finger in her mouth, moving it up and down like a brush. She had just finished rinsing her mouth when she heard Calvin's door open.

"Oh, sorry," he said, stopping in the hall when he saw her.

"No worries, I'm done," she said. She could feel his eyes on her as she passed him in the hall and returned to the master bedroom.

Sydney looked up briefly at Dani as she entered but made no effort to move to greet her. "You tired too, girl?" Dani asked as she gave the dog a quick pat before climbing into bed. It wasn't the most uncomfortable bed and once she recovered from the movement of getting into it, the pain in her ribs dulled enough that she could sleep.

11

C alvin woke early the next morning. He pulled on a new pair of pants and changed his shirt before opening the door to his room. Surprise flooded him as he realized Dani's door was open. Was she already up?

The smell of coffee hit him as he got closer to the kitchen, and he shook his head in wonder. Even bruised or broken ribs couldn't keep this girl down.

"Morning," she said, turning to him as he entered. "I hope you don't mind that I made some coffee."

"Not at all," he said, trying not to focus on how tempting she looked in his t-shirt. "I simply wasn't expecting to see you up and about so early."

"Well, you did say not to spend too much time lying down. I couldn't, anyway. Sleep was not my friend. So, it's a grit-through-the-pain-and-manage kind of thing. I don't know about you, but I need coffee to manage and Tylenol, but I already took that." She held up a cup and her lips pulled into a playful smile.

He returned the smile. "Agreed. Coffee is my first go-to each morning."

She pulled another mug out of the cupboard - she had obviously looked around - and poured him a cup. "There's some milk and I found some sugar," she said, "but that's all."

"That's all right. I like it black with two sugars." He took the mug, brushing her fingers with his own as he did. Her eyes flicked to his, but she said nothing.

"Well, then you're all set," she said. "I prefer a little more cream, but beggars can't be choosers."

As Dani took her mug to the table and gingerly sat down, Calvin fired up the stove and made them some eggs. He wished he had thought to bring bacon too. For some reason, he wanted to impress Dani.

"So, after breakfast," she said, after chewing a bite of eggs, "can we try to find my partner? I want to make sure he didn't get stuck. We didn't have much protective gear in the truck, and he and Dexter could be freezing."

"Dexter?" Calvin asked.

"His K-9."

"Oh, right. Are you sure you feel up for it? I doubt

my truck will make it out of the snow, so it would mean walking."

"We have to at least try," she said. "He would look for me if the roles were reversed."

Calvin should have known. Dani was one tough woman, and she would not be content to sit around and wait for her partner to find them. "All right," he agreed. "After breakfast, but you have to promise to turn back if it's too much for you."

Her eyebrow arched on her forehead. "I appreciate your concern, but I can take care of myself."

"I have no doubt of that," he said with a laugh, "but you did have a tree fall on you yesterday."

"Not the whole tree," she said with a crooked smile.

Calvin's heart thudded in his chest as their eyes locked. He couldn't remember the last time a woman held his interest like this, but of course it would be a woman he shouldn't date.

"Right," she said, breaking the connection. "I'll go get dressed then, and we can head out."

"Sure," Calvin said. He should not feel disappointed. She was here on a job, not to hang out with him. And her job was to arrest his brother, which made it even more ridiculous to be attracted to her. His shoulders heaved, and he stood, picking up their plates and taking them to the sink.

Dani entered a few minutes later, back in her dark BDUs. "Ready?" she asked.

"Almost," Calvin said. He walked to the hall closet and pulled out a heavy coat for her. "You'll never make it without one."

Her lips folded into a tight line as if she were about to argue with him, but with a sigh, she nodded and pulled the coat on. "I wish I had something of Aaron's. Sydney would be able to track him if I did."

"There's only one road out of here," Calvin said as he put on his own coat. "If he stayed on the road, we'll find him."

"Aaron is a rule follower," she said. "He'll be on the road. Sydney, come."

"So, how long have you been partners with Aaron?" Calvin asked as they exited the cabin. He hoped he didn't sound jealous.

"About six months. I started working with him while training Sydney. He's great, but we're kind of in different places. I mean, he'll be retiring soon, and I'm just getting started."

"Oh." A feeling of relief flooded Calvin, but he didn't know what else to say. His communication skills were failing him right now. He opted for a change of conversation instead. "This way."

A quiet stillness filled the air. On any other day, Calvin would have loved it, but today it just emphasized the awkwardness between the two of them. Was she attracted to him as well?

They walked in silence for a while - the only sounds her labored breathing and the crunching of snow beneath their feet. As they got closer to road though, Calvin grew worried. The road wasn't very traveled this far out, so he shouldn't hear anything, but the soft hum of machinery floated in the air. That typically only meant one thing - something had covered the road.

In spring, that meant a mudslide as the snow melted too quickly and sent rocks and mud tumbling down the hill. In the winter, it usually meant a small avalanche although due to the most recent storm, it could also mean several downed trees. Either way, it might mean another few days at the cabin. Although he wouldn't mind the time with Dani, it brought its own challenges as he had only brought enough food for a few days for himself. With two of them eating, the supply would disappear much faster.

Suddenly, he heard a thump behind him. He turned to see Dani crumpled in the snow. "Dani?" he hollered and rushed to her side. Her eyes flitted to his, glazed and unfocused. "Dani? Can you hear me?" When she still didn't respond, Calvin snaked his arms beneath her and lifted, curling her to his chest carefully so as not to damage her ribs any further. Her head fell against his chest, sending her blonde hair cascading down his arm. She was heavy, but not unmanageable. However, he was glad they hadn't gone much farther.

Sydney looked up at him with worried brown eyes. "It's okay, girl. We'll get her back to the cabin."

The walk was slow, partly due to her dead weight in his arms and partly because he checked every step before stepping fully. He did not need to fall and make Dani's situation worse.

Calvin sighed with relief when the cabin came into view. Though he worked out, his arms felt like jello at the moment, and he wasn't sure how much longer he would have been able to carry her. He nudged the door open with his hip, thankful he hadn't locked it when they left and then laid Dani down on the couch.

Her face was pale and clammy. With a gentle touch, he brushed her hair from her forehead and started at the heat coming off her. He unzipped her coat and pried her arms out of the sleeves with a careful deliberateness. Sydney lay her head on the couch beside Dani.

Calvin tried to think back to his time as an EMT intern. He hadn't seen a lot of broken ribs, but he didn't think a fever was a good thing. It probably meant an infection. He would have to lower her fever quickly as he had no way to get her to a hospital.

Calvin hurried to the bathroom and pulled a washcloth from the closet. He ran it under cool water and then returned to Dani. Her eyes flashed open as he laid the cloth on her head, but he didn't think she saw him.

He pulled his cell from his pocket and turned it on. He'd shut if off when he arrived and saw there was no service and no electricity. His hope was that would conserve the battery until cell service was restored. The light flickered, and his phone came to life, but 'No Service' still stared at him from the upper corner. Calvin sighed, closed all his applications, and set his battery on power saver mode. He would pray and hope service was restored soon.

12

D ani's head felt hot. No, not just her head. She felt hot all over. And cold. So cold. Where was she? She struggled to open her eyes, but they were like lead. A hand touched her fore-head, her cheek. Who was that? Aaron? No, he had left her to get help when the tree fell. Calvin? But why? They had been walking to find Aaron and then… What happened then?

Something wet touched her arm. Sydney? She tried to lift her arm, but it too did not respond.

"Oh, thank God."

The voice belonged to Calvin. At least she thought it did. It sounded fuzzy and she found it hard to concentrate.

"My name is Calvin Phillips. I'm located in a cabin at …" The words faded away for a moment. "… Injured

K-9 officer and her dog with me… bruised or fractured a rib, but now she is unconscious and running a fever. The snow is too high … Can you send help?"

Fever? That would explain the hot and cold sensation she was experiencing. What did that mean though?

"Dani?" His voice was near her. If she could make her eyes work, she believed she would see his face inches from hers. "If you can hear me, Dani, hang on. Help is on the way." His hand again touched her forehead, moved her hair, squeezed her hand. If only she could tell him she was okay.

"DP?" Was that Aaron's voice? How did Aaron get here? Was she dreaming? "What did you do to her?"

"Do to her? I rescued her from the fallen tree and warmed her up. She seemed fine this morning and then she wanted to try to find you. She collapsed in the snow, and I carried her back."

"You shouldn't have let her go."

"Yeah, you try telling her that."

Hands touched her forehead, her wrist. Other voices spoke, but Dani focused all her energy on listening to Aaron and Calvin.

"We need to move her now." Whose voice was that?

"You're coming with me." Dani knew that tone. Aaron meant business.

"Fine, as long as I can check on Dani afterwards."

"I think you've done enough."

"You can't stop me."

"Watch me."

She wanted to tell them to stop fighting, to explain to Aaron that Calvin had helped her, but still nothing seemed to follow her commands. Arms grabbed her feet and under her arms, lifting her up and placing her down on something hard. A stretcher? Pressure fell across her forehead, her feet, and her waist. Then, the sensation of moving.

The cool air hit her, and she shivered. They were outside? A whirring, chopping sound reached her ears.

"We'll take her in the chopper. You can meet us at the hospital."

Chopper? They had flown in a chopper for her?

"What about my car?"

"We'll come back for it when I'm through with you."

Dani tried one more time to speak, to tell Aaron he had it all wrong, but it was still no use. As the stretcher moved closer to the chopping noise, darkness overcame her once again.

13

"Is she going to be okay?" Calvin asked as he followed the officer to the SUV.

Officer Jones turned angry eyes on him as he opened the back door and loaded the dogs. "She might be, but if anything happens to her..."

"I did my best," Calvin said, cutting the officer off.

"You shouldn't have moved her." The slamming door punctuated his sentence. Pain was evident in the officer's voice. He must care for Dani. Were they more than partners?

"If I hadn't she would have died of hypothermia," Calvin shot back.

"The road was closed. I couldn't get back."

"And I couldn't call for help until I had service."

The two men stared at each other for a moment in a silent stand-off. Then, Officer Jones sighed and ran a hand across his chin, stubbled black and grey. "I'm sorry. I'm just worried about her."

"Me too," Calvin said before opening up the passenger door and climbing inside. He wondered if he should admit that. If Officer Jones had feelings for Dani, he wouldn't stand in the way. They would share a bond he would never be able to match.

"Why?" Officer Jones asked as he slid in the driver's side and inserted the key into the ignition. The engine roared to life, and the SUV pulled out slowly, crunching over the snow. "I mean our job was to arrest your brother and maybe even you. Why would you care what happens to her?"

"Well, first off because I'm a decent human being," Calvin said, bristling at the inference the officer was implying. "But also because I spent time with her. She's smart and stubborn, and she bested me at Scrabble."

"Yeah, DP will do that," Officer Jones said with a smirk.

"Why do you call her DP?" Calvin asked with narrowed eyes. "She told me her name is Dani."

"It is. Danielle Pascale to be exact, but she goes by Dani to sound more like one of the guys. I wanted to call her something different, however, and DP kind of stuck."

"Pascale? Is she French?" Calvin asked.

"No, her mom simply loved the name," Officer

Jones said with a laugh. Then, his smile dropped and his lip folded in. "Look, I understand you saved her, but I still have to ask. Do you have any idea where your brother is?"

Calvin shook his head. "No, as I told Dani, I went to the cabin hoping he would show up there, but he didn't. I don't want Chris to go to jail, but I'm not hiding him from you."

Officer Jones nodded. "That's good."

The men drove on in silence. Calvin wanted to ask the officer if he and Dani were involved. It was obvious he cared for her, but he also appeared much older. The grey in his hair and beard led Calvin to believe he was in his late forties or early fifties and Dani looked closer to thirty. Of course, Calvin knew age didn't always matter in love, but even though he didn't know Dani well, he couldn't see her dating her partner.

"She's special, you know?"

"What?" Calvin asked. The statement had come out of left field.

"If you're thinking about pursuing her, you need to understand she's special."

"Oh, I wasn't…" Calvin stumbled over his words.

Officer Jones fixed a steely gaze on him. "I'm not blind, man. I can see there's an attraction." He turned his gaze back to the road. "Just make sure it's more than a simple attraction before you make a move. DP needs someone who will be there for her. She hasn't had much male stability in her life, and the last thing she needs is someone looking for a good time."

"I'm not that type of guy," Calvin said.

"Good."

The silence fell again, but Calvin's mind continued to spin. So, Officer Jones and Dani weren't together, and it sounded like she was single. But did he want to pursue something with her? She was still an officer looking for his brother. And he didn't even know if she was interested. He needed time. Time to sort through these crazy thoughts banging around in his head. But he also needed to see her to make sure she was okay. And soon.

14

D ani opened her eyes and then immediately shut them. The light shone so brightly. Where was she?

"DP?"

Dani swiveled her head to the right where Aaron's voice came from. "It's too bright," she whispered.

"What?"

"The lights... too bright." Her voice sounded scratchy and soft.

"Oh, right." Footsteps shuffled across the floor and returned. "Is that better?"

She opened her eyes, blinking a few times to get used to the light, but at least this time they remained open. "Water? Can I have water?"

"Right." He grabbed the cup sitting on the table

near the bed and held it out to her. After a few sips of the straw, the scratchy sensation in her throat subsided.

"Where am I?" she asked though she discerned it was a hospital. The white bed with silver rails and the sterile environment of the walls gave her that much information. She wondered which one.

"Gorge River Hospital. Evidently, you collapsed trying to walk out to find me. Calvin carried you back and called 911 when service was restored. We choppered you out."

"Why did I collapse?" Her chest still seemed tight, every breath a chore.

"An infection in your lung. One of your broken ribs punctured it and when you went gallivanting around, the infection spread."

"I was looking for you," she said. "I feared you were trapped out in the snow. There was no gear in the car."

"You still shouldn't have done it," Aaron said. "I understand you aren't supposed to stay in bed with broken ribs, but a mile hike in knee deep snow is not taking it easy."

"I'm sorry," she said. "Where's Sydney? Is she okay?"

"Yeah, she's with Dexter at my house. Calvin said she never left your side."

"And Calvin?" She didn't really want to ask, afraid

that her attraction would show in her voice and on her face, but she needed to know.

"He's fine. I took him in for questioning. He's with the lieutenant now."

"Oh." He hadn't come to see her. She wasn't sure why she had expected him to. Sure, he had cared for her in the cabin, but probably only out of a sense of obligation.

"Disappointed?" he asked, and Dani sensed the teasing tone in his voice.

"No, I simply wanted to thank him is all."

"Right." Aaron pursed his lips and nodded. "You felt no attraction to him whatsoever."

Heat crawled up Dani's neck as she thought about Calvin's handsome face. She wasn't usually attracted to men with beards, but she couldn't deny she felt something for him. Plus, she held vague memories of him sitting with her, of the concern in his voice and the gentleness in his touch.

"Maybe a little," she said, "but it doesn't matter. It would never work. We're after his brother. That's no way to start a relationship."

"Perhaps not, but DP, if there is something there, don't you owe it to yourself to try?"

"Are you trying to marry me off?" Dani asked with a small laugh. The chuckle sent another wave of pain through her, and she hugged her ribs.

"Yes, I am. Mags is getting jealous, and I need to assure her there's nothing between us."

"Stop." Dani smiled at his antics. Margaret - or Mags as he called her - was Aaron's wife and the least jealous person Dani knew. In fact, she often invited Dani over to their house to share dinners since she knew Dani's family wasn't close by.

"Seriously though. I think he might have feelings for you as well. Though I gave him the old 'You hurt her I kill you' speech."

Dani gasped. "Aaron, you didn't."

"Well, not exactly like that, but I made him aware he needed to be serious if he was attracted to you. You need a solid guy, DP, one who will treat you right."

"Thanks, Aaron. You're a good partner. Now when can I get out of here?"

Aaron chuckled and shook his head. "Same old DP. Not for a few days, I'm afraid. They want to monitor the infection and make sure everything is healing before they release you. Even then, you'll be on restricted duty another few weeks."

Dani sighed. It was what she had figured, but she didn't want to be stuck in the hospital or at home or even at a desk doing modified duty. She wanted to be out with Sydney catching the bad guys and saving the good ones.

"I have to get back to work," he said, checking his watch, "but I'll swing by later with some food from Mags. She was adamant that hospital food wasn't good enough for you and planned to cook up a storm today."

"You have an amazing wife, Aaron," Dani said as he stood.

"I know." He walked to the door and then turned back to her. "You could have a fantastic marriage too, DP. You just need to be open to possibilities." Then he pulled open the door and exited the room.

Possibilities. Could they exist with Calvin? She had certainly felt comfortable around him, and she had enjoyed the camaraderie they shared. The fact that he loved Scrabble was a plus and he didn't seem to mind dogs. But he was a Christian, and she... well she wasn't sure what she was, but she did want what Aaron and Margaret had. She wanted a husband and kids, the American dream. But would she find it with Calvin?

15

"Thanks for the ride," Calvin said to the officer who dropped him off at the cabin. Officer Jones had taken him in for questioning but after an hour, the police released him, convinced he wasn't hiding his brother. For all the trouble Chris was bringing him, Calvin wasn't sure who would be harder on Chris - the police or himself.

He unlocked the cabin door and stepped back inside. Since Chris hadn't shown up and the road had now been cleared, no reason to stay any longer remained. Besides, he needed to return to work, but a final stop remained before he could do that. He didn't know if they would even let him in, but Calvin needed to see Dani - to make sure she was okay.

As he passed the couch, he picked up the blanket he had covered Dani with and folded it. A soft flowery scent wafted up from it and Calvin smiled. Among other things, he did enjoy the way Dani smelled, even in her BDUs. He placed the blanket on one corner of the couch and headed down the hall to the room he slept in the previous night. His bag sat on the dresser where he had left it. In no time at all, he gathered up his clothes and repacked the bag.

From there he ventured into the kitchen and packed the last of the perishable food - milk and a few eggs. With those secure in his bag, Calvin gave a final glance around the cabin. Everything was as it had been when he arrived a few days previously although a little cleaner. He should remember to come back more often after the snow melted. It wasn't that he didn't like snow but being stuck with no way to get help when Dani needed it had made him enjoy it a little less. Thankfully, the service had been restored in time. The other possibility was simply too devastating to imagine.

He slung the bag over his shoulder and opened the front door. The air was still crisp and cold, the ground still covered in white. It was a beautiful sight and one he wouldn't mind sharing with Dani again one day if she were amenable and once she was healed.

Calvin shook his head as he locked the cabin door. He was getting ahead of himself as he didn't even know if Dani was interested. However, the hospital was only half an hour away, so he would find out soon.

THE GORGE RIVER HOSPITAL was a small, one-story white building that looked more like a large office park than a hospital. Calvin wondered if Dani was really getting the best care here as he pulled into a space and parked the truck.

A single nurse manned the desk in the main room and Calvin approached her, putting on his best smile. "Can you tell me which room Officer Higgins is in?"

"I'm not supposed to release that information," the nurse began hesitantly.

"Please. I was the one who called 911 and stayed with her until they came." Calvin had often been told he possessed puppy dog eyes and he used them to his advantage as he turned them on the nurse, a pretty brunette who appeared to be in her early thirties.

A soft pink blush seared her cheeks as she returned his gaze. "Oh, all right," she said. She tapped the keys on the computer and then looked back up at him. "She's in room 119, just down the hall."

"Thank you," he said and flashed her a disarming smile before continuing the direction she pointed. As he neared 119 though, his confidence waned. What would he say to her? Would she even want to see him?

"Lord, help me know what to do," he asked silently as he pushed the door open.

Dani lay in the hospital bed, her blond hair fanning out on her pillow. "Care for some company?" he asked, knocking softly on the door.

She turned her eyes from the TV to meet his, and they lit up. Relief flooded him, and he stepped farther in. "Calvin, I'm so glad you stopped by. I wanted to thank you."

His heart dropped. Thank him. Of course. "You're welcome," he said, stepping closer to her bed and letting the door close behind him. "I'm just glad to see you looking better. How long until you're released?"

Her nose scrunched in disgust. "Two more days, but then I have to take three days off and be on modified duty for another two weeks."

"And I'm guessing that's a bad thing," he said slowly.

She chuckled. "I don't do still. I mean when I get off work I guess I do - drink some wine while Sydney and I watch TV, but that's about it. I much prefer action."

Calvin smiled. He may not know her well, but he already understood she didn't like being still. "Well, when you're stuck at home the next few days, are you required to stay at home?"

"What do you mean?" she asked, her voice laden with curiosity.

"Just that if you're not required to stay home, maybe we could do something - low key, of course. I don't want your partner's wrath poured out on me again."

"He poured out his wrath on you?" Dani asked, her lips tugging into a smile.

"Yeah, read me the riot act for letting you go hiking that morning. I told him I tried to tell you no, but that you are one stubborn woman."

This time a full smile appeared on her face. "I am that, aren't I?"

"Yes, you are. So, what do you say?"

"I say yes," she said, and this time when her eyes twinkled, he believed it was for him.

"Good." Calvin smiled. He glanced around the room, looking for paper or something to write his number on for Dani.

"What do you need?" she asked.

"A pen and paper. You know where I live, but I thought it might be better if we discussed plans over the phone rather than you having to show up at my house to contact me."

Dani chuckled softly. "Why don't I just give you my number and you can text me. That way I'll have your number too. Or if you'll get my phone from my bag over there, I can put it in now."

"Right, of course," Calvin said, feeling like a fool as he pulled out his phone. "Give me a second to get to the right screen." His finger fumbled with the screen as he tapped the one to get to text messages. "Okay, I'm ready."

"360-999-7632," she said.

"Okay, got it," Calvin said. "I'll let you get your rest, but let me know when you get out, and we'll plan something."

"Sounds great."

DANI WATCHED Calvin leave and wondered what she was doing. Yes, Calvin's handsome looks sent her heart racing, and he was certainly in shape if he carried her back to the cabin. He'd be able to keep up with her without a doubt, and she had enjoyed his company, but she was still actively looking for his brother. Well, *she* wasn't actively looking, but her fellow officers were. Could a relationship survive that?

"Hey, DP, you look like you're trying to solve the world's problems. What's up?"

Dani shook her head and smiled at Aaron, who had snuck into the room - a feat for him at six feet and two hundred pounds. "I was just thinking. Calvin came to see me…"

"Oh, yeah?" he asked, cutting her off. He set the cloth bag he carried on a table and began pulling out containers. "And?"

"And he sort of asked me out," she continued.

Aaron's right eyebrow shot up his forehead. "How do you sort of ask someone out?" He opened the container in his hand, took a deep breath, and smiled. "Cinnamon apples, my favorite."

"Well, I told him about my confinement to my house upon release and he offered to get together to combat the boredom."

Aaron's forehead furrowed with tiny lines. "Uh, I might have been out of the dating scene for a while, but I'd say his technique needs some work."

Dani laughed and then grabbed her chest when the pain erupted. "Don't make me laugh. Yeah, it might, but I think maybe he was nervous. The thing is though, do you think it could work? I mean his brother is still a person of interest."

"Are you planning to date his brother?" Aaron asked as he opened another container.

"No," Dani said. "What sort of question is that?"

"Well, you aren't planning to date his brother and you can't work on the case for another month, so I don't see the big deal. We'll probably find him while you're on leave, and you'll never even have to be involved. Maybe the brother won't even be the shooter, and we won't have to arrest him."

"Yeah, I guess you're right," Dani said, but uncertainty remained. Perhaps her own dysfunctional family experiences clouded her view. She wasn't sure Eric would forgive her if she ever had to arrest Derek or vice versa, but Aaron could be right. Maybe since she would no longer be the arresting officer anyway, it would matter less.

"That smells delicious," she said, deciding to push the conundrum away for now. "What did Margaret send?"

"Orange chicken, stir-fried vegetables, and cinnamon apples for dessert."

"You really are a lucky man," Dani said as she took the proffered container and fork.

"I know," Aaron said with a smile before loading up his fork with food.

16

Calvin paced the house, checking for the third time to make sure everything appeared clean and put away. He was generally a neat person anyway, but some days, when work took over, housecleaning took a back seat and piles began to build. Since he'd spent the first day catching up on work, the piles had built up enough he'd had to take the morning off to clean up today.

The doorbell rang, and he took a deep breath as he crossed to the door. He had offered to pick Dani up, but she had insisted on meeting here. He didn't know if she was just being cautious or if perhaps she was hiding something, but as he opened the door, he wasn't sure he cared anyway. She was here. On his doorstep and willing to hang out with him. Of course, his lame proposal of "planning something" made it so he wondered if this were a date or just friends getting together, but still she was here. She looked adorable in her brown leather jacket, scarf, and yellow hat - like a ray of sunshine in the middle of winter.

"Hi," she said. "I hope you don't mind that I brought Sydney. She's starting to get stir crazy just like me."

"No, it's fine," he said, mentally scrapping his plans of taking her out on a paddleboat. He had picked a paddleboat, so he could take her out on the water, but make sure she didn't exhaust herself. However, dogs weren't allowed on paddle boats. Evidently, there had been a rash of them jumping into the middle of the water and having to be rescued. And even though Sydney was a K-9 and probably better trained, he wasn't sure the marina would make an allowance. "There's a great park about a mile from here. Do you want to take her there to let her run around and then we can get some lunch?"

"That sounds fun," Dani said.

"All right, shall I drive?" he asked.

"Actually, can we take my car? It's got a hook up for Sydney's leash."

"Sure." He pulled the door shut and locked it before following her to a small SUV. She opened the back door and commanded Sydney to jump in. Once situated, she clipped the leash onto a hook on the side.

"That must make your job easier," he said.

She nodded. "Yeah, it does. I mean Sydney is great about staying back here anyway, but it makes me feel like she's a little safer when I drive. I guess it's kind of like knowing your kid is strapped in, you know?" She pushed a button on the underside of the door and it closed.

"I don't have any kids," he answered with a laugh, "but I see your point."

"Me either," she smiled, "but that's what I hear, anyway."

Calvin opened the passenger door and sat down, reaching for the seat belt.

"You want any?" Dani asked.

"Kids?" Calvin asked, turning to face her.

Her eyes dropped to her lap and she fumbled with the keys. "Yeah," she answered, but she didn't look at him.

"I would love kids one day. What about you?"

"Yeah, I think so," she said, shoving the keys in the ignition. "I mean I like kids, but my mom was a serial divorcer, so I'm not sure I'd even know how to be a good mom." The engine fired up, and Dani backed the car out, still never looking Calvin's way.

He wasn't quite sure what to say to her, but he felt the need to say something. "I think you would be a wonderful mother."

She glanced at him and smiled before turning her attention back to the road.

DANI SMILED as Sydney scampered back and forth at the park. The exuberant dog had clearly been inside too long.

She sneaked a glance at Calvin who stood a few feet away watching Sydney run. "Thank you for this," she said. "I know you probably had something else planned."

"It's no big deal," he said. "We can do what I planned another day. That is if you want to see me again."

"I would definitely enjoy seeing you again." She smiled and then looked away. Why was she being so bold? Not that she never made the first move, but she still knew little about Calvin. However, something about him set her at ease. He was a calming presence, something she hadn't felt in a long time.

AFTER THE PARK and a bite to eat, Dani turned the car back toward Calvin's house, but she found she didn't really want the night to end. She wanted to spend more time with him. She wanted to kiss him. Though she'd tried to keep her mind off the thought, his lips had filled her head multiple times today.

"Would you like to come in?" Calvin asked as she parked the SUV. "The night is still early. We could watch a movie or something."

Dani's heart leapt. It was like he was reading her mind. "You have *The Princess Bride*?"

He gaped at her as if she had two heads. "Do I have *The Princess Bride*? Of course, I have *The Princess Bride*, woman. It's a cult classic. Just because I liked the book better doesn't mean I didn't buy the movie."

Dani chuckled at his comment, careful not to laugh too hard, and opened her door. "Let's go then, but you better have some popcorn too."

"Oh, I got popcorn."

A smile played across Dani's face as she rescued Sydney from the back and followed Calvin into the house. She enjoyed walking slightly behind him as the view from behind was just as nice as the view from the front.

With the door unlocked, he opened it and gestured her inside. She had been here before, but her focus had been consumed with the task of looking for Chris. Now, she took the time to really observe the place.

The room was sparse but decorated nicely. Few pictures hung on the wall, but the ones he had chosen were classy - black and whites. His furniture all matched and was a soft tan color, and the couch faced a big screen tv.

"Popcorn, right?" he asked, leading the way to the kitchen after shutting the front door.

"Yes, with butter, please." She motioned for Sydney to stay and then followed Calvin into the kitchen. It too was decorated neatly. The counters were void of clutter and held only a toaster, a coffee pot, and a Vitamix blender.

He opened the pantry and pulled out a bag of microwave popcorn. A few minutes later, the smell of butter and salt filled the air and the soft popping of the kernels dwindled. Calvin opened the microwave door before it beeped and then turned to her.

"Can you grab a bowl from that cabinet there?" he asked, pointing to a lower cabinet to Dani's left.

She squatted down and pulled a large silver bowl from the cabinet. Then, she placed it on the counter and Calvin poured the steaming popcorn into it.

"Okay, I guess we're ready," he said.

"I think I might need to taste it first," Dani said, popping a kernel into her mouth.

"Hey, cheater. Save it for the movie." Calvin picked up the bowl and held it against his chest, blocking her from grabbing any more kernels.

"No fair," she said, tugging at his arm. "I'm injured, remember?"

"That doesn't seem to be stopping you," he said with a laugh.

When they reached the living room, he handed the bowl to her. "I can't believe I'm doing this. Don't eat it all before I get some too."

Dani smiled a mischievous smile and sat in the corner of the couch, watching as he rifled through DVDs until he found the right one. He popped it into the player and then joined her on the couch.

He was less than a foot from her, but it was enough of a distance that no part of them was touching and Dani fought the urge to scoot closer. It didn't even have to be much - his thigh against hers or a touch of their shoulders, but he made no move to sit closer. With a small sigh, Dani settled for the occasional touch of their fingers when they both reached into the bowl at the same time.

When the movie began, Dani tried not to repeat the lines with the characters. It was a bad habit of hers, but when Calvin began uttering the lines as well, she stopped holding back. It became a competition to see who could repeat the most lines, and Dani was surprised he knew the movie as well as if not better than she did. She tried to keep her heart in check as she was sure something about Calvin she didn't like would emerge, but for the moment things were perfect. In fact, she couldn't remember a time when she had enjoyed hanging out with someone more.

Somewhere in the middle of the movie, the popcorn ran out. Their fingers touched as they both scraped the bottom of the bowl. In unison, they turned to each other and the moment arrived. Dani held her breath as Calvin's eyes bore into hers, silently seeking permission to kiss her. Her lips parted in answer, and she saw the corner of his lip pull up in a smile. Dani closed her eyes as his hand cupped her chin. His thumb traced a slow circle on her cheeks sending goosebumps across her flesh, and then his lips touched hers. Soft and firm, his lips pressed into hers.

"Well, that was…."

"Amazing?" she suggested.

"Yeah," he breathed. He opened his mouth to say more, but the alarm on Dani's phone interrupted him.

"I'm sorry," she said, silencing the alarm. "It's my reminder to wind down so I can be alert for work the next day. I guess I don't really need it tonight, but I should probably get going anyway."

"Yeah, I need to get some sleep before work tomorrow too, but can I see you again?"

"I'd love that," Dani said, and she tried not to think about how much she wanted to kiss him again.

∾

CALVIN'S LIPS were still tingling from the kiss when the knock at the door sounded. A smile crossed his face. Had she changed her mind? Was she back for more?

"Dani, I..." the words froze in his mouth as he opened the door. It was Chris on the other side of the door and not Dani. Calvin glanced around to make sure Dani was gone and no one was watching.

"Hey, Calvin can I come in?"

Calvin hesitated, not sure if he should let Chris in or not. He didn't seem high, more scared. "The cops are looking for you, Chris."

Chris's eyes shifted to the left and right and he scrunched deeper into his coat. "I know, man, and I'll turn myself in, but can I tell you what happened first?"

Calvin knew he should say no. With the police looking for Chris, he should turn him away and call Dani himself, but he wanted to hear Chris's side. It wasn't that he didn't trust the cops, but he'd watched enough shows to know that people not strong in their story could be made to change it. At least if he heard the story first, he'd have a way to help Chris, even if in just a small way.

"Okay, but only for a minute. Long enough to hear your story, and then I drive you in myself."

Chris nodded. "Sure, Cal, whatever you say."

Calvin stepped back and let Chris enter before shutting the door behind him. "Okay, speak."

"I messed up bad this time, Cal. I got involved with this guy who thought we could take on the dealer. He brought a gun, but the dealer's crew had guns too. I don't know how it happened, but it hit the fan, you know? Bullets went flying and one of the dealer's crew ended up dead. We ran, but we kept the drugs, or the other guy did. Now the dealer's crew is out for blood. They're after me, but I don't have the drugs and the other guy's gone missing. I don't know what to do, Cal."

"I'll tell you what we're gonna do. I'm going to call my friend Dani and you're going to go in with her. Tell her everything you just told me and help them take the dealer down. You'll probably still have to serve some jail time, but maybe they can get you a lesser sentence." He patted his pockets looking for his phone, but it wasn't there. He must have left it in the kitchen. "I'll be right back," he said to Chris.

Calvin headed into the kitchen, scanning the counters. Where had he left his phone? The bare counters stared back at him, devoid of his cell phone and giving no hints as to where it might be. If he hadn't left it in the kitchen, had he lost it somewhere else? He could use the landline, but he didn't have Dani's number memorized, and he wanted to tell her first.

"Help me find my phone," he said as he walked back to the living room, but silence greeted him. Chris was gone. Calvin sighed. He had been so close to helping him. With heavy shoulders, he collapsed onto the couch and there stuck in the couch cushions was his phone.

17

"You seem awful chipper today," Aaron said as he unwrapped the sandwich Dani brought him. She was still off duty for another day, but she couldn't just sit at home, so she'd brought Aaron lunch. Dexter and Sydney sat chewing on bones a few feet away.

"I did have a nice evening last night," Dani said, fighting the blush that threatened to grace her cheeks as she thought of the shared kiss the night before.

"Oh yeah?" Aaron's eyebrow arched, and his eyes begged for details.

"Okay, I spent the day with Calvin. We went to the park and let Sydney run around. Then we ate dinner and then we returned to his place and watched a movie."

Aaron's eyes narrowed. "Uh huh, that all sounds

nice, but I heard nothing to be so glowing about. So what else happened?"

Dani rolled her eyes. "All right, we kissed."

"Uh huh, now that's what I'm talking about. When are you seeing him again?"

"Tonight. He needed to work this morning, but he's cooking me dinner at six," Dani said.

"Sounds like you like this guy," Aaron said.

"I do, except..." Dani paused.

"Except what?"

"Except he's pretty religious, and I'm not sure I want to do that again, you know?"

"DP, I know you had a bad experience, but not every Christian is like your ex," Aaron said.

Dani snorted and drew a pattern on the table with her finger. "Yeah, I met James at church if you remember."

"Look, James had issues. He shouldn't have cheated on you. That was wrong, but at least you found out before you married him. It could have been much worse, and that was God looking out for you."

"I never thought of it that way," Dani said.

Aaron shot her a pointed look. "Now, I don't know this Calvin well, but he appeared a decent fellow when I spoke with him. Maybe you could give him and God another chance."

"Yeah, maybe," Dani said. She finished her sandwich in silence, but Aaron's words bounced around in her brain. She had blamed God, not that she'd been much of a Christian before James, but attending church with him opened her eyes to a father figure she'd never experienced. However, when James cheated on her, she blamed God and left the church, but maybe Aaron was right. Maybe God showed her James's true colors to keep her from marrying him. If that was the case, she owed him a giant apology.

There was a church on her way home and Dani decided to stop in and have a few quiet moments with God. As she unloaded Sydney though, the dog jerked to the right.

"What is it, girl?" Dani asked.

Sydney's response was to whine and pull on her leash some more.

"Okay, girl, let's see what's got you so riled up." Dani gave the dog a little slack and followed where she pulled. To the right of the church was an alley. The hair on Dani's neck stood up as Sydney led the way into the darker area.

The alley was empty except for a dumpster which Sydney made a beeline toward. As Dani cleared the side of the dumpster, she saw why. A man lay crumpled in a heap on the ground and if Sydney had alerted, it could only be one man. His face was pale, but even without its normal color, the resemblance to Calvin was unmistakable.

Dani leaned down and checked for a pulse. Weak, but there. She turned her attention to the rest of the man. Blood pooled around his midsection where it looked he had been stabbed several times.

Dani pulled out her phone and dialed 911. Then she took a deep breath and dialed Calvin's number. He picked up on the second ring. "Calvin? It's Dani. It's about Chris. Can you meet me at St. Michael's downtown?"

"What is it?" he asked, and fear was palpable in his voice.

"He's been stabbed. I've called an ambulance, but I think you need to be here too."

The response was a click and then silence, but Dani didn't blame him. Worry for his brother was his main concern right now. She lowered the phone and returned it to her pocket.

The ambulance and Calvin arrived at approximately the same time.

"What happened?" Calvin asked as he watched the EMTs load Chris up into the back of the ambulance.

"I don't know," Dani said, touching his arm. "I found him like this."

"I should have called you when he left last night," Calvin said, running a hand through his hair.

"What?" Dani's guard instantly shot up.

"After you left last night, he stopped by, told me his story. I was going to call you and drive him in myself, but I couldn't find my phone. While I was looking, he slipped out."

"You should have called me anyway, Calvin," Dani said.

"I understand, and I'm sorry. Is he going to be okay?" Calvin looked back toward the ambulance.

"I'm not sure. Why don't you go with them and I'll meet you at the hospital soon? I can take your statement there," Dani said. The cop in her was irritated he hadn't called her when Chris came by, but the civilian in her understood and realized that right now he needed to be there for his brother.

"Thank you," he said. He squeezed her hand, gave her a final longing glance, and then climbed into the back of the ambulance.

His haunted brown eyes were the last thing Dani saw before the doors closed. As the ambulance drove away, she led Sydney back toward the front of the church. She still had unfinished business inside, and now it seemed she needed to pray for Chris too. The stab wounds had looked deep and she wasn't sure he would live through the night.

18

Calvin paced the hospital floor waiting for word from the surgeon. Chris had been stabbed multiple times in the abdomen and at least one vital organ had been hit. They had rushed him into surgery shortly after they arrived.

"Any news yet?"

He turned to see Dani approaching him, and a wave of emotion swept over him. She must have noticed it as she wrapped her arms around him and laid her head on his chest. With that simple gesture, the tears that Calvin had so carefully held back flooded his eyes and spilled down his cheeks.

"He's all that I have left," he said into her hair. "I know he's messed up, but he's all that I have left."

She squeezed him tighter and nodded against his chest. "It will be okay."

"Calvin Phillips?"

Calvin turned to see a man in blue scrubs standing a few feet away. His heart dropped to the floor. "Yes, I'm Calvin."

"I'm Dr. Rhodes. I'm the surgeon who operated on your brother. We managed to stop the bleeding, but his liver and spleen were both injured. His liver should heal on its own, but his spleen was ruptured. I repaired it, but we'll need to watch it closely to make sure it heals properly."

"He's going to be okay, then?" Calvin asked. Dani dropped her arms and stepped away, and while Calvin appreciated the gesture, he missed her warmth and comfort.

"Well, there's always a risk with surgeries, but he's stable for now."

"Can I see him?"

The doctor hesitated. "For a few minutes, but he needs to get his rest."

"I need to get your statement after anyway," Dani said. "Go ahead and see him and I will be here waiting when you get back."

"Thank you," Calvin said before following Dr. Rhodes down the hallway.

Chris looked pale in the hospital bed. His eyes were closed, and tubes flowed from his arms.

"He's sleeping and probably won't wake while

you're here. We gave him drugs for the surgery and pain killers."

"He's an addict," Calvin said. "Did you give him anything that is addictive?"

"No, but thank you for the information. We'll put an extra watch on him in case he starts to detox," Dr. Rhodes said. "Five minutes, no more, okay?"

Calvin nodded and stepped closer to the bed. Dark shadows circled Chris's eyes and his cheeks were sunken in, but he looked peaceful. It was the most peaceful Calvin had seen him look in ages.

"Hey, little brother," he said, "I'm sorry this happened to you, but maybe this will be what you need to get your life back on track. I hope this hiatus will help you get off drugs."

Chris didn't respond, but his chest rose and fell in a regular rhythm and that was enough for Calvin for now. After saying a quick prayer for Chris's recovery, he squeezed Chris's arm and then exited the room and walked back to where Dani was waiting. "I don't know how much help I'll be, but I'm ready to give my statement now."

DANI WANTED TO ASSURE CALVIN, to tell him everything would be all right, but the truth was she didn't know.

She had no idea what charges might be filed against Chris or what his future might hold. Calvin's statement wasn't much to go on, but it held hope that perhaps there was someone bigger the police might want to go after.

"Do you want to get some dinner?" she asked as they finished.

Calvin shook his head. "Can you just take me home?"

Dani nodded, but she wanted to do more. It hurt her heart that he was hurting.

As they drove, she thought back to her moment in the church earlier. She had asked God to forgive her for pushing Him away and she'd felt lighter, not so jaded. Now, she asked for wisdom in what to do. How to help Calvin, and as they pulled into his parking lot, one word settled on her shoulders. Pray!

"Calvin," she said as they reached his door, "can I pray with you?"

He turned questioning eyes on her. "I thought you didn't pray."

"I didn't," she said with a soft smile. "Then someone reminded me that sometimes things happen for God to save us from something worse. I'll tell you the rest of my story one day, but right now I'd like to pray with you for Chris."

A wet sheen covered Calvin's eyes as he nodded.

"Thank you, I would like that."

Dani followed him inside and asked for the words to say. She hadn't prayed aloud in ages, and to be honest, the thought terrified her.

"What's going to happen to him?" Calvin asked as they sat on his couch.

Dani shook her head. "I'm not sure, Calvin, but he's a small fish in the big sea of drugs. My guess is they will offer a reduced sentence in exchange for information on the dealer, but only if he can and will give them the information."

"Can you be there when they ask him?" Calvin asked. "I know it's probably not your case anymore, but I'm worried he'll say what they want him to say. Can you be there?"

"I'll try," Dani said, squeezing his hand. "Can I pray for him now?"

Calvin nodded and closed his eyes and Dani let the words come to her. It was strange that as she ended, she didn't feel awkward or weird. Was that because she had let God lead or was it because she felt so comfortable with Calvin?

"Thank you," he said when she finished. "I know we didn't meet under the best circumstances, but I'm really glad you're in my life."

"Me too," she said. She locked eyes with him and ran her hand down his bearded cheek before leaning in and brushing his lips with her own. "I should go, but I'll call you tomorrow?"

"I'd like that," Calvin said.

19

C hris was awake when Calvin entered the hospital the next day.

"Hey, little brother. How are you feeling?" Calvin asked.

Chris offered a weak smile. "Like I've been stabbed."

"Yeah, do you remember what happened?"

"I should have let you take me in that night," Chris said, "but I was scared. So, I ran. I made the mistake of going home and they were waiting for me. I managed to get away the first time, but they followed me and caught me by the church. Do you know who found me?"

Calvin nodded. "Yeah, my friend Dani. She's a K-9 officer, and I've asked her to be there when they question you. But, Chris, you might still face jail time."

"I know," Chris said, "and I'll deserve it, but will you come visit me?"

"Of course I will," Calvin said. "You and me, we're family. No matter what happens."

"Cal, do you think God will still accept me?" Chris asked. His face was serious, and his eyes were clear of drugs. It was the first time Calvin had seen him this way in a long time.

"You know he will," Calvin said. "You just have to ask him."

"Can you help me?"

Calvin smiled and squeezed Chris's arm. "I'd be happy to."

CALVIN WAS STILL in high spirits when he picked Dani up for their date that night. "Guess what, Dani? Chris came back to Jesus today." He picked her up and swung her around.

"That's great, Calvin," Dani said with a smile. "I have good news too."

"Oh yeah?" he asked as he set her down.

She nodded and her smile reached from ear to ear. "I talked to the DA and asked if they would consider pursuing rehab as an option for Chris, and they agreed. He will have to stay in for six months instead of the regular three, but he won't have to serve any jail time."

Calvin's heart stopped in his chest. This was more than he could have hoped for. "Dani, that's great."

"I know, right?"

"You really are amazing," Calvin said, pulling her closer to him.

Her arms wound around his neck, and her smile turned into a mischievous smirk. "I think you're pretty amazing too, Calvin Phillips."

When his lips touched hers, Calvin felt an emotion he hadn't felt in a long time. Not since his parents' death, and in his heart, he knew that Dani was the woman he would marry someday.

"Whoa, what's with the smile?" Aaron asked as Dani picked up Sydney that night after her date with Calvin. He often watched her when Dani didn't want to board her or leave her alone too long. She returned the favor by watching Dexter whenever he needed her to.

"This wouldn't be about the new man, would it?" Margaret asked with a sly smile as she came up behind Aaron. Margaret was a quiet woman with graying hair but twinkling blue eyes. Though in her fifties, she still seemed young at heart.

"Maybe," Dani said with a smile.

"Oh, I think that's more than a maybe," Margaret said, jabbing Aaron. "I think we might be attending a wedding sooner than you think."

"A wedding?" Aaron asked. "Margaret, she's only known him a week."

"I knew you were the one after our first date," Margaret said, looking up at Aaron. "It took longer for you, of course." She leaned closer to Dani and lowered her voice. "Men are blind sometimes." She patted Aaron's arm and smiled at him. "Now, you should get to know this guy to make sure, but when God sends you the right one, you just know."

Dani smiled. Though she hadn't necessarily been thinking about him being "the one," she couldn't deny she had pictured the future with him. They had so much in common, and he possessed a strength she found extremely attractive, but could she really know after just a week and some days. Was that possible?

"I'll keep that in mind," Dani said. "Thanks again for watching Sydney."

"Always a pleasure," Aaron said. "See you tomorrow at work?"

"Yep, bright and early," Dani said. As she took Sydney's leash and said goodbye, she couldn't help smiling. She had another date with Calvin after work tomorrow and as far as she was concerned, the time could not go fast enough.

20

F our months later, Calvin stood over the jewelry case looking at rings. On one hand, he couldn't believe he was about to do this, but on the other, he couldn't believe he hadn't done it sooner. Every day he spent with Dani just solidified his feelings for her.

She had begun attending church with him, and afterwards they would go to Chris's rehab facility and spend the afternoon with him. During the week, they shared dinner and devotionals together and took Sydney out for evening walks if the weather wasn't too bad. Thankfully, it was now late spring, and the rain showers were tapering off as summer grew closer.

"Do you have an idea what you're looking for?"

Calvin's eyes flicked up to the salesman who regarded him with kind eyes behind a small pair of spectacles. He wore a brown suit that matched the color of his mustache.

"Yeah, something special," Calvin said.

"Well, I expect that," the man said with a small smile. "Do you have anything in mind?"

Calvin scanned the rings again. Dani had delicate hands. She would need something small so as not to look gaudy. Also, in her line of work, it was probably important that it not affect her job. At the far corner of the case, he spied a ring he thought would be perfect. A shiny diamond sat in the middle of the setting and smaller diamonds lined the ring on either side of the center diamond.

"That one," he said pointing. "Can I see it closer?"

"Ah, that's a good choice," the man said as he pulled it out. "It's a half carat all together with the main diamond being just over a quarter and the other diamonds filling out the rest."

The man continued to rattle off something about color, cut, and clarity, but Calvin didn't understand all of it. What he knew though was when he held the ring, he pictured it on Dani's finger.

"This one. This is the one," he said.

"Excellent," the salesman said. "Let me wrap it up for you."

After handing over his credit card and signing the receipt, Calvin slipped the ring box into his pocket. He patted that pocket as he walked out, enjoying the promise of what that box might hold. That was if she said yes.

As he stepped into the sunshine, his smile stretched across his face. The only thing that would make the day any better was if Chris could be here with him, but he had another two months in rehab. However, he would be out in time for the wedding. As long as Dani accepted his proposal.

DANI REGARDED herself in the mirror and smoothed down the simple black dress she had just pulled on. It was the third dress she had tried on and she still wasn't sure it was the right one. What was wrong with her tonight? Why was she feeling so undecided?

"What do you think, Sydney? Is this the one?"

Sydney glanced up from her bone, but her brown eyes held no approval or rejection.

"You're right," Dani said, "I should change." But before she was able to pull the dress off, a knock sounded at her door. "Drat, I guess this will have to suffice."

With a final glance in the mirror and a small sigh, Dani walked through the house to the front door. Calvin stood on the other side wearing a button down green shirt that made his hazel eyes appear more green than brown and holding a bouquet of flowers.

"Wow, you look amazing," Calvin said.

Heat flared up Dani's neck, and her eyes dropped to the floor. "Thank you. Come on in. I need to get Sydney taken care of before we go." She took the flowers from him and stepped back to allow him in.

After a quick stop in the kitchen to put the flowers in some water, Dani continued to the bedroom where Sydney was still finishing her bone.

"Okay, girl, time to get in your crate."

Sydney's eyes regarded her, but the dog made no effort to move.

"Come on, Syd, it's only for a few hours," Dani cajoled as she patted the crate.

Sydney let out a soft huff, but she picked up her bone and walked into the metal crate.

"I promise I'll let you out as soon as I get back," Dani said with a smile as she shut and locked the door. Then she turned her attention to Calvin. "All right, I'm ready."

Calvin held out his hand and Dani took it, enjoying the pulse that shot up her arm. Even four months later, his touch still elicited sparks.

He held the truck door open for her - another trait that Dani found charming, before shutting her door and climbing into the passenger side.

"Where are we going for dinner?" she asked.

"You'll see," he said with a sly smile.

Dani's heart skipped a beat in her chest.

Fifteen minutes later, Calvin pulled into a spot in front of Falls Terrace. The restaurant was one of the pricier ones in town mainly due to the beautiful view of the waterfall out its back wall which was solid glass. As they entered the building, Dani couldn't help wondering what he had in store.

The host led them to a table closest to the glass. Calvin pulled out her chair, pushing it into the table as she sat. Then he took his seat across from her. Dani didn't know which the better view was - the lights on the waterfall outside or Calvin sitting across from her.

"Welcome to Falls Terrace," the waiter, a young man clad entirely in black, said as he approached the table. "Can I get you something to drink?"

"Can we have a bottle of your finest red wine?" Calvin asked.

The waiter smiled and nodded before turning away from the table to retrieve the wine.

"Wine, huh? Is this a special occasion?" Dani asked with a teasing tone.

"It's always a special occasion when I'm with you, but yes tonight is more special than other nights. I have a very important question for you."

As he rose from his chair, Dani's heart surged into

overdrive. A minute later, his knee was on the floor in front of her. Dani's breath caught in her throat. Though she had hoped for this moment, she had not expected it to arrive so quickly.

Calvin reached into his pocket and pulled out a small velvet box. "Dani Higgins, I know it hasn't been long, but I can't imagine you not in my life. Will you do me the honor of becoming my wife?"

He popped the lid open and tears sprung into Dani's eyes. The ring was small, but one of the most beautiful she had ever seen. She wanted to answer yes, but her throat was constricted with emotion. All she managed was a nod, but it was an enthusiastic one as Calvin took the ring out of the box and slid it onto her finger.

As he leaned in to kiss her, clapping and cheering erupted around them. Dani couldn't remember a time she had been happier.

21

"You sure you want to go through with this?" Chris asked as he straightened his tie in the mirror.

"Very funny, little brother," Calvin said, coming up behind him and throwing an arm about his shoulder. Now that Chris was clean and sober, the resemblance between the two brothers was much greater. Chris was clean shaven, but they shared the same hazel eyes inherited from their mother and the same strong nose and chin their father passed to them.

"You know I'm only kidding," Chris said. "Dani is amazing. I hope I find a woman like her soon."

"You will," Calvin said, patting Chris's shoulder. "Remember, you're kind of starting fresh, but you have a new job, a new home, a church, us, and most importantly God on your side. He will send you the right woman when it's time."

Chris had been out of rehab for six months. Around the second month, Calvin managed to find him a position with his company. Together, they fixed up Chris's old house to salvage some of his deposit, and Chris moved in with Calvin. He would soon be the sole owner of Calvin's house as Calvin and Dani had decided to live in her house after the wedding.

"You're right. I'm so glad I got the chance to start over again. Okay, you ready to get married?"

"Absolutely," Calvin said with a smile. He had waited for this moment for eight long months. Originally, they planned to wait only until Chris was out of rehab, but then Dani decided she wanted to get married a year from the day they met which added another few months. He hadn't minded too much though as it gave them time to get everything else settled and in order. And really, as long as Dani became his wife, he would have waited as long as it took.

"You have the rings?" Calvin asked Chris.

"Yep, right here." Chris patted his pocket and the two headed out to take their place in the sanctuary.

The small church was nearly filled to capacity between their church friends and Dani's friends in the department, but Calvin only vaguely registered them. His gaze was fixed on the back door of the sanctuary, where any moment, the woman he loved would appear.

The music started, and the back doors opened. Gabby, Dani's half-sister, entered first. She was pretty much the opposite of Dani with darker hair and a fuller figure, but Calvin was still glad she'd come. Dani had worried her family wouldn't show, but her mother and both her half-brothers made the trip as well. It warmed Calvin's heart to see them rekindle their relationship over the last few days, and he hoped they would continue to get together after the wedding.

Gabby smiled at him as she reached the front and then took her place on the opposite side of the preacher. The music changed then, and Calvin's breath caught in his throat as Dani entered the sanctuary. Her blond hair was pulled up in some sort of elaborate updo with only a few tendrils curled around her cheeks.

She glided forward like an angel. The dress she'd chosen showed off her slender shoulders and pooled out around her feet in a satin train that made it appear as if she were walking on a cloud.

As she reached the front, she handed her bouquet to Gabby and took his hands. Just like the first time they touched, his heart sped up as their skin met.

"Dearly beloved," the pastor began, "we are gathered here today to join this man and this woman in holy matrimony."

Dani smiled as Calvin squeezed her hands. She couldn't believe the moment was finally here or that her family showed up. The last few days had been amazing as she spent time with them and caught up on their lives.

"Do you, Calvin, take Dani to be your lawfully wedded wife? To have and to hold? Through sickness and in health? As long as you both shall live?"

"I do," Calvin said.

"And do you, Dani, take Calvin to be your lawfully wedded husband? To have and to hold? Through sickness and in health? As long as you both shall live?"

"I do," Dani said, not bothering to contain the smile spreading across her cheeks.

"Then by the power vested in me by God and the state of Washington, I now pronounce you husband and wife. You may kiss your bride."

At those words, Dani's smile stretched even further. She had waited a long time to hear them and she didn't want to waste another moment kissing Calvin as her husband for the first time.

He winked at her as he pulled her to him and

seared her lips with a kiss. Though the kiss itself was short, it held the promise of much more to come in a few hours and a heated blush spread up Dani's cheeks.

"I can't wait till this evening," Calvin whispered in her ear.

"Me either," Dani returned, "but right now we better get to the reception."

"Whatever you say, Mrs. Phillips," Calvin said as he took her hand and led her down the aisle.

Mrs. Phillips! Though new and different, she enjoyed the sound of it. As she passed Aaron and Margaret on the way out, she couldn't help thinking about how much her life had changed in just one short year and how she owed it all to one all-powerful God and one former drug addict. He really did work in mysterious ways.

The End!

IT'S NOT QUITE THE END!

Did you enjoy — Lawfully Redeemed? If you did, please leave a review. It really helps. http://books2read.com/Lawfullyredeemed

You won't want to miss the other books in the series!
Turn the page for a sneak peek!

22

AUTHOR'S NOTE

First off, let me say how glad I am that you read this book. Lawfully Redeemed was a lot of fun to write though again I had to research how they trained K9 dogs.

This was the first book I set close to where I live now. Being from Texas, I place a lot of my books there because I lived there for twenty-eight years and the saying is really true. You can take a girl out of Texas, but you can't take Texas out of the girl. Even though I've now lived in the Pacific Northwest half the time I lived in Texas, I still feel that Texas is my home.

Don't get me wrong, there are some amazing things you can do here that you can't do in Texas like….. hang out under trees lol. Lots and lots of trees. Hiking and skiing and kayaking. All things you would have to drive pretty far to do from where I grew up in Texas. But, I still miss the thunderstorms and my family of course.

But I digress. My point was it was fun to write about something closer to home, and I have a few more books out and coming that will also be set in Washington state.

So if you've enjoyed reading this author's note so far (and really, how could you not?) I am offering, for today only, a page where you can sign up for my weekly newsletter for the low, low price of absolutely nothing.

Included in this weekly newsletter are many wonderful things like pictures of my adorable children, chances to win awesome prizes, new releases and sales I might be holding, great books from other authors, and anything else that strikes my fancy and that I think you would enjoy.

Even better, I solemnly swear to only send out one newsletter a week (usually on Tuesday unless life gets in the way which with three kids it usually does). I will not spam you, sell your email address to solicitors or anyone else, or any of those other terrible things.

Join me here and receive a free novella as my thank-you gift for choosing to hang out with me. It's fun and entertaining. I promise.

Prayers and blessings,

Lorana

NOT READY TO SAY GOODBYE YET?

Calvin's and Dani's story is done for now, but I've had many readers ask me to give Chris a story, so it will probably come soon. Until then though let's take a look at my other contemporary lawkeeper romance, Lawfully Pursued.

This book I love for two reasons. Jesse, the hero, is based off a friend of mine at my gym. I even asked him what he would have on his walls in his house. It's always fun to bring in people from my life and change them up a bit for fiction, but he really is a boxer (a darn good one too) and a total sweetheart. Second, this is my first billionaire book. Brie isn't technically a billionaire but the daughter to one and it definitely got me started on my Sweet Billionaires Series.

Enjoy a little look at Lawfully Pursued!

Lawfully Pursued

HE ISN'T LOOKING **for a fling...**

Unlike some of his single buddies, Jesse wants something more out of life, so he is not impressed with Brie when he first meets her. However, after spending time with her, he begins to see her in a new light.

She's a spoiled rich girl looking for some fun...

Brie Carter is bored of her life, but her decision to spice it up with a bet will have unforeseen consequences when she begins to fall for the sweet SWAT agent

All bets are off....

When Jesse finds out he was just a target for her boredom. Will she be able to convince him she's changed?

Read on for a taste of Lawfully Pursued....

24

LAWFULLY PURSUED PREVIEW

B rie Carter fell back spread eagle on her queen-sized canopy bed sending her blond hair fanning out behind her. With a large sigh, she uttered, "I'm bored."

"How can you be bored? You have like millions of dollars." Her friend, Ariel, plopped down in a seated position on the bed beside her and flicked her raven hair off her shoulder. "You want to go shopping? I hear Tiffany's is having a special right now."

Brie rolled her eyes. Shopping? Where was the excitement in that? With her three platinum cards, she could go shopping whenever she wanted. "No, I'm bored with shopping too. I have everything. I want to do something exciting. Something we don't normally do."

Brie enjoyed being rich. She loved the unlimited credit cards at her disposal, the constant apparel of new clothes, and of course the penthouse apartment her father paid for, but lately, she longed for something more fulfilling.

Ariel's hazel eyes widened. "I know. There's a new bar down on Franklin Street. Why don't we go play a little game?"

Brie sat up, intrigued at the secrecy and the twinkle in Ariel's eyes. "What kind of game?"

"A betting game. You let me pick out any man in the place. Then you try to get him to propose to you."

Brie wrinkled her nose. "But I don't want to get married." She loved her freedom and didn't want to share her penthouse with anyone, especially some man.

"You don't marry him, silly. You just get him to propose."

Brie bit her lip as she thought. It had been awhile since her last relationship and having a man dote on her for a month might be interesting, but.... "I don't know. It doesn't seem very nice."

"How about I sweeten the pot? If you win, I'll set you up on a date with my brother."

Brie cocked her head. Was she serious? The only thing Brie couldn't seem to buy in the world was the affection of Ariel's very handsome, very wealthy, brother. He was a movie star, just the kind of person Brie could consider marrying in the future. She'd had a crush on him as long as she and Ariel had been friends, but he'd always seen her as just that, his little sister's friend. "I thought you didn't want me dating your brother."

"I don't." Ariel shrugged. "But he's between girlfriends right now, and I know you've wanted it for ages. If you win this bet, I'll set you up. I can't guarantee any more than one date though. The rest will be up to you."

Brie wasn't worried about that. Charm she possessed in abundance. She simply needed some alone time with him, and she was certain she'd be able to convince him they were meant to be together. "All right. You've got a deal."

Ariel smiled. "Perfect. Let's get you changed then and see who the lucky man will be.

A tiny tug pulled on Brie's heart that this still wasn't right, but she dismissed it. This was simply a means to an end, and he'd never have to know.

JESSE CALHOUN RELAXED as the rhythmic thudding of

the speed bag reached his ears. Though he loved his job, it was stressful being the SWAT sniper. He hated having to take human lives and today had been especially rough. The team had been called out to a drug bust, and Jesse was forced to return fire at three hostiles. He didn't care that they fired at his team and himself first. Taking a life was always hard, and every one of them haunted his dreams.

"You gonna bust that one too?" His co-worker Brendan appeared by his side. Brendan was the opposite of Jesse in nearly every way. Where Jesse's hair was a dark copper, Brendan's was nearly black. Jesse sported paler skin and a dusting of freckles across his nose, but Brendan's skin was naturally dark and freckle free.

Jesse flashed a crooked grin, but kept his eyes on the small, swinging black bag. The speed bag was his way to release, but a few times he had started hitting while still too keyed up and he had ruptured the bag. Okay, five times, but who was counting really? Besides, it was a better way to calm his nerves than other things he could choose. Drinking, fights, gambling, women.

"Nah, I think this one will last a little longer." His shoulders began to burn, and he gave the bag another few punches for good measure before dropping his arms and letting it swing to a stop. "See? It lives to be hit at least another day." Every once in a while, Jesse missed training the way he used to. Before he joined the force, he had been an amateur boxer, on his way to being a pro, but a shoulder injury had delayed his training and forced him to consider something else. It had eventually healed, but by then he had lost his edge.

"Hey, why don't you come drink with us?" Brendan clapped a hand on Jesse's shoulder as they headed into the locker room.

"You know I don't drink." Jesse often felt like the outsider of the team. While half of the six-man team was married, the other half found solace in empty bottles and meaningless relationships. Jesse understood that - their job was such that they never knew if they would come home night after night - but he still couldn't partake.

Brendan opened his locker and pulled out a clean shirt. He peeled off his current one and added deodorant before tugging on the new one. "You don't have to drink. Look, I won't drink either. Just come and hang out with us. You have no one waiting for you at home."

That wasn't entirely true. Jesse had Bugsy, his Boston Terrier, but he understood Brendan's point. Most days, Jesse went home, fed Bugsy, made dinner, and fell asleep watching TV on the couch. It wasn't much of a life. "All right, I'll go, but I'm not drinking."

Brendan's lips pulled back to reveal his perfectly white teeth. He bragged about them, but Jesse knew they were veneers. "That's the spirit. Hurry up and change. We don't want to leave the rest of the team waiting."

"Is everyone coming?" Jesse pulled out his shower necessities. Brendan might feel comfortable going out with just a new application of deodorant, but Jesse needed to wash more than just dirt and sweat off. He needed to wash the sound of the bullets and the sight of lifeless bodies from his mind.

"Yeah, Pat's wife is pregnant again and demanding some crazy food concoctions. Pat agreed to pick them up if she let him have an hour. Cam and Jared's wives are having a girls' night, so the whole gang can be together. It will be nice to hang out when we aren't worried about being shot at."

"Fine. Give me ten minutes. Unlike you, I like to clean up before I go out."

Brendan smirked. "I've never had any complaints. Besides, do you know how long it takes me to get my hair like this?"

Jesse shook his head as he walked into the shower, but he knew it was true. Brendan had rugged good looks and muscles to match. He rarely had a hard time finding a woman. Jesse on the other hand hadn't dated anyone in the last few months. It wasn't that he hadn't been looking, but he was quieter than his teammates. And he wasn't looking for right now. He was looking for forever. He just hadn't found it yet.

Continue reading Lawfully Pursued!

25

A FREE STORY FOR YOU

Enjoyed this story? Not ready to quit reading yet? If you sign up for my newsletter, you will receive Once Upon a Star, the love story of Blake and Audrey, two of my Star Lake characters, right away as my thank you gift for choosing to hang out with me.

Once Upon a Star

A high school crush....

Blake was a nerd in high school. Never noticed. Looked over. So, it was no wonder that Audrey paid no attention to him, but now that she's back in town...

Audrey left Star Lake to pursue acting, but when she ends up pregnant and alone, she finds herself forced to return home.

Can Blake show Audrey a new side? Will she trust him enough to stay?

Read on for a taste of Once Upon a Star....

26

ONCE UPON A STAR PREVIEW

A udrey tried to peek around the nurses leaning over the silver table, obscuring the view of the thing she wanted to see most.

"Are you ready, Mom?" The head nurse, a kind, older woman with just a touch of gray in her dark hair, turned to Audrey, a tiny blue package in her arms.

Mom. The word had never applied to her, and she wasn't sure it fit. Was she ready? Probably not. Would she ever be completely ready? Probably not. But that didn't change reality. She tucked a strand of blond hair behind her ear and nodded.

"Here's your son." The nurse held the swaddled bundle out to her. Audrey opened her hands, unsure of what the nurse wanted her to do. The nurse's face softened and her warm brown eyes sparkled. With one hand, she adjusted Audrey's arms to place the tiny bundle in them. "Hold him like this." She demonstrated the proper technique. "You always want to support his head."

Audrey nodded, trying to keep her arms from shaking. She was afraid to breathe, afraid to move, but mostly afraid she'd drop the infant, so she kept her eyes glued to him. Would he shatter like a piece of glass? The image sent a shiver down her spine. She didn't want to find out.

The nurse's eyes twinkled as she watched Audrey adjust and readjust her holding position. "There is a bassinet here." She pointed at a clear plastic tub that looked like a large shoe box on top of a wheeled table. It didn't look comfortable to Audrey, and she wondered how a baby slept in it. "If you want to take him walking, you need to put him in the bassinet, okay?"

"Do I hold him the rest of the time?" As much as she was enjoying the baby in her arms, what happened when she needed to sleep or use the bathroom?

The woman chuckled. "You hold him as much as you want and put him down when you need a break. We'll come in every few hours to check on you, and we'll show you how to change his diaper and dress him. You'll be a pro before you know it. Don't worry." She patted Audrey's arm like her grandmother used to when she asked a silly question, and then the nurse walked out of the room, still smiling and shaking her head.

Audrey's eyes dropped to the sleeping baby. His shock of dark hair reminded her of his father, the olive-skinned Italian who had charmed her with his fast tongue. She hoped it was the only trait Cayden would get from him. The world didn't need another heart-breaker. "I have no idea what we'll do, Cayden, but we'll figure something out."

BLAKE TURNED the glass on the countertop and glanced up at Max who leaned against the back counter, arms folded across his chest as if he were waiting for the answer to a question. The green of his plaid shirt matched the faded ball cap turned backwards on his head. "Sorry, did you say something? I'm distracted; it's just getting close to Christmas, and I miss Connie." A vision of the day she left popped into his head.

Blake opened the door, expecting to see Connie on the other side in her Sunday best. The church service started in half an hour. Though Connie stood there, his smile faded as he took in her jeans and t-shirt. There was no requirement of the patrons to dress up, but Connie always wore a dress or skirt. "What's going on?" Blake asked.

Connie bit her lip and her eyes fell to the ground. "I wanted to say goodbye."

"Goodbye?"

"I can't stay any longer, Blake." Her eyes lifted to meet his, and he saw the shimmer of liquid in them. "I hoped I could make a life here, but I'm a city girl. I miss the lights and night life. I miss the excitement."

"But, we were discussing marriage last week." Blake struggled to make her words compute in his brain.

"I know," she nodded, "and that's what got me thinking. The thought of living the rest of my life here is depressing, so though I love you, I have to say goodbye." She leaned in and pecked his cheek before flashing a sad smile and walking back to her car.

With a heavy heart, Blake watched her drive away before shutting the door and leaning against it. His brain tried to make sense of her departure.

"I get it," Max said, leaning forward and dispersing Blake's memory. "It's not the same, but you're welcome to spend Christmas with Layla and me.

Blake offered a half smile. "I'll consider it, but it's your first Christmas together. You've been in love with that woman since I've known you and I don't want to be a third wheel. Besides, I'll probably hit the Christmas Eve service at church and spend the day with my mom. She's been lonely without my father around."

Max shrugged and turned back to the kitchen to finish serving the lunch crowd.

Blake took a bite of his hamburger, but while he knew it was delicious—Max was known for his burgers—it held no taste in his current mood. He fished a few dollars out of his wallet, laid the money on the counter, picked up his coat, and walked out the door.

The McAllister development where he worked sat a mile up the road, but as he still had fifteen minutes remaining on his lunch break, he decided to walk through downtown. His own house resided on the quiet outskirts of town, so other than hanging out with Max at The Diner, he didn't spend much time in the downtown area.

Blake pulled his coat tighter as the winter air bit through the heavy wool. Star Lake generally received one or two good snowfalls every winter, and though Christmas was still a few weeks away, the chill in the air made him believe the first snow was coming.

He didn't mind the snow, but he enjoyed it more when he had someone to share the experience with. Curling in front of the fireplace alone held little appeal.

AUDREY SHOVED the last item in her suitcase and pushed down on the bulging bag as she tugged on the zipper.

"Where are you going to go?" Desiree asked, leaning against the doorframe.

Desiree was Audrey's roommate, and the two were about as different as night and day. Where Audrey was pale and blond, Desiree had darker skin and long dark hair.

"The only place I can," Audrey said with a sigh. "Home."

The thought held little appeal. Her wealthy parents had given her access to her trust fund at eighteen, and Audrey had opted to move to LA to try her hand at acting. At first, it had been fun. She'd found a few jobs and been in a few commercials, but then the jobs had become fewer and farther between, and after she ended up pregnant, they had dried up completely. Now all the money she had saved was almost gone.

Desiree's nose scrunched in disgust. "You'd go back to that tiny town, why?"

"I haven't had a job in months Dez, my savings have run out, and I can't go to work without someone to watch Cayden. If I go home, I can get help from my parents until I get back on my feet."

At least she hoped they would help. They hadn't been too happy when she decided not to go to college, but she didn't think they would turn their grandson away, even if they didn't want to help her.

Desiree shrugged and flicked her hair behind her bony shoulder. "Nothing in the world would make me return to my crappy hometown."

Audrey knew Desiree's home life had been rough, but while she hadn't wanted to grow up under her mother's thumb, it hadn't been a bad childhood. "I don't know if I'll ever be back, but I wish you luck."

After a quick hug, Audrey picked up Cayden's car seat, slung her bag over her shoulder, and left the apartment she had called home for the last few years.

Click here to sign up for my newsletter and continue reading Once Upon a Star.

WOULD YOU LEAVE A REVIEW?

As an author, I highly appreciate the feedback I get from my readers. It helps others make an informed decision before buying my book. If you enjoyed this book, please review at your retailer.

THE STORY DOESN'T END!

You've met a few people and fallen in love....

I bet you're wondering how you can meet everyone else.

Star Lake Series:

When Love Returns: The first in the Star Lake series. Presley Hays and Brandon Scott were best friends in High School until Morgan entered their town and stole Brandon's heart. Devastated, Presley takes a scholarship to Le Cordon Bleu, but five years later, she is back in Star Lake after a tough breakup. Brandon thought he'd never return to Star Lake after Morgan left him and his daughter Joy, but when his father needs help, he returns home and finds more than he bargained for. Can Presley and Brandon forget past hurts or will their stubborn natures keep them apart forever?

Once Upon a Star: The second book in the Star Lake series. Audrey left Star Lake to pursue acting, but after an unplanned pregnancy her jobs and her money dwindled, leaving her no option except to return home and start over. Blake was the quintessential nerd in high school and was never able to tell Audrey how he felt. Now that he's gained confidence and some muscle, will he finally be able to reveal his feelings? Once Upon a Star will take you back to Christmas in Star Lake. Revisit your favorite characters and meet a few ones in this sweet Christmas read.

Love Conquers All: Lanie Perkins Hall never imagined being divorced at thirty. Nor did she imagine falling for an old friend, but when she runs into Azarius Jacobson, she can't deny the attraction. As they begin to spend more time together, Lanie struggles with the fact Azarius keeps his past a secret. What is he hiding? And will she ever be able to get him to open up? Azarius Jacobson has loved Lanie Perkins Hall from the moment he saw her, but issues from his past have left him guarded. Now that he has another chance with her, will he find the courage to share his life with her? Or will his emotional walls create a barrier that will leave him alone once more? Find out in this heartfelt, emotional third book (stand alone) in the Star Lake series.

The Heartbeats Series:

Where It All Began: Sandra Baker thought her life was on the right track until she ended up pregnant. Her boyfriend, not wanting the baby, pushes her to have an abortion. After the procedure, Sandra's life falls apart, and she turns to alcohol. Her relationship ends, and she struggles to find meaning in her life. When she meets Henry Dobbs, a strong Christian man, she begins to wonder if God would accept her. Will she tell Henry her darkest secret? And will she ever be able to forgive herself and find healing? Find out in this emotional love story.

The Power of Prayer: Callie Green thought she had her whole life planned out until her fiance left her at the altar. When her carefully laid plans crumble, she begins to make mistakes at work and engage in uncharacteristic activities. After a mistake nearly costs her her job, she cashes in her honeymoon tickets for some time away. There she meets JD, a charming Christian man who, even though she is not a believer, captures her interest. Before their relationship can deepen, Callie's ex-fiance shows back up in her life and she is forced to choose between Daniel and JD. Who will she choose and how will her choice affect the rest of her life? Find out in this touching novel.

When Hearts Collide: Amanda Adams has always been a Christian, but she's a novice at relationships. When she meets Caleb, her emotions get the best of her and she ignores the sign that something is amiss. Will she find out before it's too late? Jared Masterson is still healing from his girlfriend's strange rejection and disappearance when he meets Amanda. She captivates his heart, but can he save her from making the biggest mistake of her life? A must read for mothers and daughters. Though part of the series and the first of the college spin off series, it is a stand alone book and can be read separately.

A Past Forgiven: Jess Peterson has lived a life of abuse and lost her self worth, but when she is paired with a Christian roommate, she begins to wonder if there is a loving father looking down on her. Her decisions lead her one way, but when she ends up pregnant, she must make some major changes. Chad Michelson is healing from his own past and uses meaningless relationships to hide his pain, but when Jess becomes pregnant, he begins to wonder about the meaning of life. Can he step up and be there for Jess and the baby?

Sweet Billionaires Series:

The Billionaire's Secret: Maxwell Banks was the

ultimate player until he found himself caring for a daughter he didn't know he had. Can he change to become the role model she needs? Alyssa Miller hasn't had the best luck with past relationships, so why is she falling for the one man who is sure to break her heart? Though nearly complete opposites, feelings develop, but can Max really change his philandering ways? Or will one mistake seal his fate forever?

A Brush with a Billionaire: Brent just wanted to finish his novel in peace, but when his car breaks down in Sweet Grove, he is forced to deal with a female mechanic and try to get along. Sam thought she had given up on city boys, but when Brent shows up in her shop, she finds herself fighting attraction. Will their stubborn natures keep them apart or can a small town festival bring them together?

The Billionaire's Christmas Miracle: Drew Devonshire is captivated by the woman he meets at a masquerade ball, but who is she? Gwen Rodgers is a teacher, but when she pretends to be her friend and meets Drew at a masquerade ball, her world gets thrown upside down.

The Billionaire's Cowboy Groom: Carrie Bliss finally found the man she wants to marry but there's just one little problem. She's technically still married. Cal Roper hasn't seen her in years but his heart still belongs to his wife. When she returns to town requesting a divorce, can he convince her they belong together?

The Cowboy Billionaire: Coming Soon!

The Lawkeeper Series:

Lawfully Matched: Kate Whidby doesn't want to impose on her newly married brother after their parents die, so she accepts a mail order bride offer in the paper. Little does she know the man she intends to marry has a dark past, sending her fleeing into a neighboring town and into Jesse Jenning's life. Jesse never wanted to be in law enforcement, but after a band of robbers kills his fiancee, he dons the badge and swears revenge. Will he find his fiancee's killer? And when Kate flies into his life, will he be able to put his painful past behind him in order to love again?

Lawfully Justified: William Cook turns to bounty hunting after losing his wife. When he suffers a life-threatening injury, he is forced to stay in town with an intriguing woman. Emma Stewart has moved back in with her widowed father, the town doctor, but she still longs for a family of her own, so no one is more surprised than she is when she starts to develop feeling for the bounty hunter, who hides his heart of gold behind a rugged exterior. Can Emma offer William a reason to stay? Can William find a way to heal from his broken past to start a future with Emma? Or will a haunting secret take away all the possibilities of this budding romance?

The Scarlet Wedding: William and Emma are planning their wedding, but an outbreak and a return from his past force them to change their plans. Is a happily ever after still in their future?

Lawfully Redeemed: Dani Higgins is a K9 cop looking to make a name for herself, but she finds herself at the mercy of a stranger after an accident. Calvin Phillips just wanted to help his brother, but somehow he ended up in the middle of a police investigation and caring for the woman trying to bring his brother in.

Lawfully Pursued: SWAT Officer Jesse Calhoun wasn't looking for love, much less with a billionaire's daughter, but Brie is hard to ignore. Brie Carter was just looking for a little fun but when a bet goes wrong, how does she keep from losing the man she's fallen in love with?

The Still Small Voice Series:

The Still Small Voice: Jordan Wright was searching for something after she gave her son up for adoption. What she found was God, and she began receiving visions. But can she trust Him when he asks her to do something big? Kat Jameson had long been a lukewarm Christian, but when her friend dies and she begins seeing lights, she thinks she is going crazy. Then she meets someone with a message for her. Will she be able to give up control and do what is asked of her?

A Spark in the Darkness coming soon!

Blushing Brides Series:

The Cowboy's Reality Bride: Tyler Hall just wanted to find love, but the women he dated wanted more than his small-town life provided. He gets more than he bargained for when he ends up on a reality dating show and falls for a woman who is not a contestant. Laney Swann has been running from her past for years, but it takes meeting a man on a reality dating show to make her see there's no need to run.

The Reality Bride's Baby: Laney wants nothing more than a baby, but when she starts feeling dizzy is it pregnancy or something more serious?

The Producer's Unlikely Bride: Justin Miller had given up on love, but when his image needs help, he finds himself needing the aid of a stranger who just happens to be a romance writer. Ava McDermott is waiting for the perfect love, but after agreeing to a fake relationship with Justin, she finds herself falling for real.

The Soldier's Steadfast Bride: coming soon
The Cop's Fiery Bride: coming soon

Stand Alones:

Love Renewed: This books is part of the multi author second chance series. When fate reunites high school sweethearts separated by life's choices, can they find a second chance at love at a snowy lodge amid a little mystery?

Her children's early reader chapter book series:

The Wishing Stone #1: Dangerous Dinosaur

The Wishing Stone #2: Dragon Dilemma

The Wishing Stone #3: Mesmerizing Mermaids

The Wishing Stone #4: Pyramid Puzzle

The Wishing Stone Inspirations 1: Mary's Miracle

authorloranahoopes.com

loranahoopes@gmail.com

To see a list of all her books

authorloranahoopes.com

loranahoopes@gmail.com

ABOUT THE AUTHOR

Lorana Hoopes is an inspirational author originally from Texas but now living in the PNW with her husband and three children. When not writing, she can be seen kickboxing at the gym, singing, or acting on stage. One day, she hopes to retire from teaching and write full time.